THE
PORT-WINE STAIN

THE
PORT-WINE STAIN

WITH AN UNFINISHED TALE BY EDGAR A. POE

Norman Lock

Bellevue Literary Press
New York

First published in the United States in 2016 by
Bellevue Literary Press, New York

For information, contact:
Bellevue Literary Press
NYU School of Medicine
550 First Avenue
OBV A612
New York, NY 10016

© 2016 by Norman Lock

This is a work of fiction. Characters, organizations, events, and places
(even those that are actual) are either products of the author's imagination
or are used fictitiously.

Library of Congress Cataloging-in-Publication Data
Lock, Norman, 1950–
The port-wine stain : with an unfinished tale by Edgar A. Poe / by >Norman Lock.—
First edition.
pages ; cm
ISBN 978-1-942658-06-1 (trade pbk. : alk. paper)—ISBN 978-1-942658-07-8 (ebook)
I. Title.
PS3562.O218P67
2016
813'.54—dc23
2015030706

Bellevue Literary Press would like to thank all its generous
donors—individuals and foundations—for their support.

 The New York State Council on the Arts with
the support of Governor Andrew Cuomo and the
NYSCA New York State Legislature

 National Endowment for the Arts arts.gov This project is supported in part
by an award from the National
Endowment for the Arts.
ART WORKS.

Book design and composition by Mulberry Tree Press, Inc.

Manufactured in the United States of America.
First Edition

1 3 5 7 9 8 6 4 2

paperback ISBN: 978-1-942658-06-1

ebook ISBN: 978-1-942658-07-8

For Edward Renn,
Doppelgänger and Friend

True!—nervous—very, very dreadfully nervous
I had been and am; but why *will* you say that
I am mad? The disease had sharpened my
senses—not destroyed—not dulled them.

—"The Tell-Tale Heart," Edgar Allan Poe

THE
PORT-WINE STAIN

PART ONE

... I have been, in some measure, the slave of
circumstances beyond human control.
                    —"William Wilson," E. A. Poe

Camden, New Jersey, April 22, 1876

THOMAS EAKINS'S PAINTING, accounted famous by
those who can appreciate it, of Dr. Gross's clinic
at Jefferson Medical College in Philadelphia has always
given me the horrors. Not the reeking hands of the surgeons nor the raw ensanguined flesh exposed on the young
boy's thigh disturbs me—by 1875, I was inured to gory
scenes, having served in the Union army medical corps
during the War of Secession—no, it's not the blood, but
the general murk above the harshly lit operating theater
where the students sit, in attitudes of boredom or indif-
ference, observing the removal of the diseased portion of
the boy's femur, that makes me anxious. To gaze at them,
at the death masks of faces rendered brutal by smears of
paint, calls up in me a sensation of dread, as if I were
straining to raise something repellent from the lightless
depths of memory—a thing too blighted for the light of
day, belonging to nightmares or to one of Poe's ghastly
tales. That the man sitting in the third row, at the far left

side of the painting, is, in fact, me makes matters worse. I shiver to see myself depicted in that grim scene like a callow student during his first amputation.

I knew Poe, in Philadelphia. Some thirty years ago, we were often in each other's company. I was not much more than a boy. . . .

Eakins made me look ten years younger than the fifty I was—not to satisfy any vanity of my own (I have none), but to ensure that I wouldn't stand out among the young men in the gallery. In the painting, which is a large one, the hair and mustache are as you see them now, only not so grizzled, and, as you can also plainly see, my posture is poor; it belongs to a man who has carried his share of burdens, or labored under more than his share of delusions. I never did carry myself well, not even when I was a young man at large in the streets of Philadelphia, eager to make something of myself.

Have you seen the painting, Moran?

No? Well, if you have the stomach for it, which a man like you must, it's hanging in the Army Post Hospital nearby the centenary exhibition. The selection committee—backbiting gentlemen artists, most of them—consigned it to that "quarantine" rather than the public galleries, so as not to offend the lady visitors by its frankness. As I said, I've reasons of my own to dislike the painting, but something compels me to look at it. I've stood in front of that appalling canvas half a dozen times already. I'm drawn to peer into the gloom of its recesses—secret recesses, I would almost say—and wonder.

At what?

I don't know, precisely. That's the wonder of it. Oh, let's say—to say something—that I'm enthralled by what's there . . . or isn't. I—I hate the bloody thing and, at the same time, am fascinated by it. It appalls me, Moran; it scares the living daylights out of me. I mentioned the strange effect his painting has on me to Eakins. I wanted to know—in my bafflement, I almost shouted at him inside the Philadelphia Club's card room. I had to know what he meant by that noxious gloom, that mud of color—too damned drab to be called color!—in which he'd posed me with my chin on my cravat, my eye sockets black and empty, as though pecked clean by ravens. The young men ranged about me fare no better. We're, all of us, enveloped in a miasma as septic, to my mind, as the poor wretch's thighbone. The operation, by the way, had not been staged for the painting; the boy and his wound were real. I tell you, Moran, the scene was a perfect horror! No wonder the boy's mother, sitting in her black dress near the great god of the scalpel, Gross, hid her head in her arm. I can't look at the thing without shuddering.

But you don't want to hear about my hysteria—unbecoming to a medical man—or about Eakins's painting, great as it undoubtedly is. You want to hear about Edgar Poe, how I came to know him and how he initiated me into the occult.

Yes, Moran, I said "occult." Poe ushered me, as it were, to the iron door of the tomb and bid me knock. He showed me a world, ashen and forlorn, seen by greasy torchlight. He taught me the true meaning of self-effacement, the loss of one's own being in another's dream—one so vivid that it threatened the balance of my reason. His morbid curiosity, piqued by the insistence of his art, caused me to doubt my own existence. Poe, Eakins—from what I know of artists, they are an unscrupulous lot. They'll do whatever's necessary to lay open the abscesses of——

Do you believe in a soul, Moran? I do, although not as Christians do, or heathens, either, for all I know of them. I believe in the soul as it might be an organ of the body whose function is to persist beyond the body's natural span, to gain for the body a kind of fame or infamy, which is an afterlife, of sorts. As in the case of any organ, the soul can become diseased. While I knew him, he made me see—Poe did; made me understand that, unlike a bodily organ, the soul desires, even wills, its own continuance. It can be said to be the seat of will and desire and, in its necrotic state, the root of evil. Evil is *real*, Moran. I know it. A Sunday school lesson or one of Cotton Mather's gaudy rants that helped to kindle the Salem bonfires is nearer to the truth of it than a fable by Poe, Hawthorne, or Melville. Evil's a malignancy beyond the skill and scalpel of even Dr. Gross to heal or extirpate. Words are as powerless against it as a witch doctor's incantation. And yet we heed them—thrill to them—glory in their ardent particles and claim enlightenment. What's Ahab and his white whale beside the slaughter of the buffalo, *The Last of the Mohicans* beside the Cherokees' Trail of Tears, the Inquisition of "The Pit and the Pendulum" beside the lynching of a negro or the burning of a witch? A symbol is no more than a clean bandage on an ugly cut, and yet we live by them and only sometimes do we realize their falsity. A story—a hook, a barb, each word a knot—it captures us;

it captured me. A young man, I became enmeshed in one by Edgar Poe.

Strange how a vile thing can seduce our minds as well as our lower natures. The caricaturists misunderstand evil, for, more often than not, it has a pleasing face, or at least an ordinary one. Corruption is seldom visible on the faces of the living. If seen at all, it is like a ragged petticoat trailing below a fancy skirt or the painted face of a hag or whore concealing the pox. Devils do not bear the outward sign of the Beast, but wear its token like a Masonic ring. If only sin were ugly, we might be rid of it like Ireland was of its tattooed snakes.

Perhaps part of my fascination for Eakins's painting is how—perhaps unwittingly—he has laid bare the base character of a number of those men of medicine, for the most part inattentive, if not asleep, sitting slumped in the gloom above the mortal struggle being waged on the operating table. In many of their faces, I see, or think I see, brutishness—even brutality—in the slashes of paint. I've studied my own in that painting and seem to see something my shaving mirror does not give back to me—something coarse and unnerving. To read one of Poe's tales or poems is to experience a like disturbance of the mind—almost a revolt against one's own better angels. No, I dislike the products of Poe's lurid imagination even more than I do Eakins's picture. Better to spend an hour with Walt Whitman's pages: The sentiments one finds there are so very frank and wholesome. There's something almost childlike about him. Didn't you find him so?

Are you an admirer of his verses, Moran?

I thought you must be. My name's Fenzil, by the way. Edward Fenzil. I've been calling on Whitman ever since Dr. McAlister, who ordinarily attends him, came down with influenza. My office is just along Stevens Street, at Broadway. Whitman bears his infirmity bravely, as you might have expected from reading his *Leaves*. To be honest, I much prefer a poem that gallops, with a rhyme to chime the end of each stretch, like Poe's "The Raven." But I'm keeping you, Moran. You have the ferry to catch if you're to visit the Philadelphia exposition. Unless you've time to have your curiosity satisfied . . .

You are curious, aren't you? It was curiosity made me linger outside Whitman's house when you went inside. Forgive me, but it's the habit of a medical man, although it began in me before I ever thought of medicine as a profession. It was Poe who awoke in me a morbid interest in things that lie far from my own little fulcrum of influence—at least he sharpened it. So if you care to hear me out, come along to my rooms and I'll tell you a tale, with a whiskey or two to take off its chill—the same that I told to Whitman during one of Eakins's visits.

Coming?

Good! I get desperate sometimes for company.

They're friends, you know, Whitman and Eakins. My tale made an impression on them both—especially on Eakins. Afterward, he invited me to pose as one of the medical students in Gross's clinic. He said I'd lend his picture "gravity," although I can't see it myself.

I sometimes think he hoped to fix me in *paint*, to make me a captive of a world not my own but—well, I can't say whose. Not his, surely, not Eakins's, except as any artist does in pigments, clay, or words. Of the three, I mistrust words most of all. Eakins is a remarkable man. He's using Muybridge's photographic motion studies to see what cannot be seen by the eye, the better to paint life, which is rarely still. The fact remains that whenever I gaze at *The Clinic of Dr. Gross,* I feel oppressed, as though I've been translated into a form of dull and inert matter. As if I'd become ossified. The only one sitting in that dirty brume whose face shows animation—whose eyes are open and aware—is Eakins. He inserted himself into his painting: He's sitting in the first row, next to the man wearing a frock coat and wing collar, with an unruly blond mustache and glazed expression. This man, the jaded one, stands in the mouth of the tunnel leading to the operating theater while Eakins leans forward, his interest piqued, his gaze intense, even cold. His hand holds a pencil, with which he's sketching the bloody scene.

Damn this wind! My pipe's gone out. Well, we're almost there.

Eakins's picture? Monstrous thing.

There's something, too, about the tunnel he painted below the gallery: It seems lit by a distant fire whose source lies elsewhere than the world of actuality that Eakins is said to have depicted with such exactitude. One would almost call the quality of that light infernal, if this weren't 1876, in an age of science and reason. See for yourself if I'm not right. You'll be sure to view the painting, won't you, Moran? It's curious and, I think, worth the time and small effort to take it in. It seems an illustration for a story Poe might've written. Perhaps he did write it, and it's been lost. There is another. . . . He died believing I'd destroyed it. I meant to, but I couldn't bring myself to burn it on the grate.

I said that I have the sensation of being in thrall to something or someone whenever I look at myself in Eakins's painting. I think it's Poe; his influence on me has persisted all this long while since we were so often together in Philadelphia during the winter of 1844 and, once that winter, in Providence, when we visited—strange to say—another Whitman: Sarah Whitman, no relation to the Good Gray Poet. A Transcendentalist and gifted medium, Sarah was also a beauty. When Poe first saw her, she was examining an African violet for mites in her sunny front parlor. That afternoon, I attended my first séance at her house in Providence.

Here's where I have my rooms and practice. They're somewhat cramped, but adequate for a bachelor's needs. Come up. Mind your head on the gas fixture.

No, I never married. After Poe's wife died, he came near to marrying Sarah Whitman. They were engaged, and Poe—a measure of his regard—gave her his pledge of sobriety, which he couldn't keep. He was too aware of himself—of the devils that scorched him with the fire of self-knowledge and made his life a misery. He was like a cat beset by vicious boys—like the boy on Gross's table, being flayed to the bone by knives. Poor Edgar found it necessary to anesthetize himself. He couldn't have lived otherwise. As it was, he died at forty. He'd suffered the torments of hell, and God was kind to take him early. If He exists. One finds no evidence of Him in Poe's stories or in Eakins's picture, for that matter. Poe wouldn't have been happy for

long, in Providence, consorting with the Transcendental-
ists. Their spiritualism was too refined, too precious, for his
nepenthean dreams. A delicate woman, Sarah took ether
for her heart. He would have destroyed her—they would
have destroyed each other. Virginia, his waif of a wife, had
been tolerant of his foibles. She, too, died young.

Make yourself at home, Moran, while I pour us each a
rye whiskey to be going on with—unless you'd prefer wine.
I have an excellent Madeira. . . .

No? Rye it is, then. You strike me as a man who's used
to roughing it. For all your apparent youthfulness, you look
worn to the bone. I've seen it before on the faces, in the pos-
tures, of soldiers of the late war, fought to stitch up or rend
asunder the Union, as the case may be. You have the lean
and haggard appearance of a prospector or a settler.

I thought as much. After the war, I returned east and
have never left it. Yes, sir, your autobiography is written in
the lines on your face, Moran. You might have stepped right
out of Whitman's book, out of one of those poems celebrat-
ing, ad nauseam, the common man. Frankly, I don't much
care for common men, though I care for them when they're
sick, or for democracy, either, when it comes to that. Poe
died on election day, in Baltimore, having several times sold
his vote for drink—which is just as it should have been.
A great man—and I believe Edgar Poe to have been one,
though his gifts were perverse—was deserving of more than
a single vote. I'm only half in jest. Toss a rope to a drowning
specimen of the common man—a Mississippi roustabout,
say—and once he's back on land and has knocked the water
from his ears, he's liable to use it to lynch the first negro

who fails to show him his respect. I can see on your face that you find my cynicism grotesque. I'm afraid experience has spoiled what pleasure I might have taken in life as it's lived by most people.

I started to tell you about the séance. Edgar Poe, Frances Osgood, a poetess, a bald and whiskered gentleman who looked like General Burnside, a young woman with catarrh, and I sat around Sarah Whitman's dining table while she rapped out messages from the dear departed. Do you believe in a talkative dead, Moran?

You're right to do so, but I would insist that, once the dead have been summoned, we ought not to be satisfied with inanities, as if the afterlife were no more mysterious than a trip by train to Atlantic City. Of all we might've learned on that winter afternoon at Mrs. Whitman's "talking table"—the answers to questions that have vexed theologians and philosophers for millennia—we heard only tittle-tattle from the Other Side, unless you consider worthwhile the peevish complaints concerning Poe's unwholesome character and addiction to laudanum voiced, telegraphically, by Sarah's late husband, John. He was clearly prejudiced against Poe and held him in contempt, in spite of John's having been himself a poet. Envy, I suppose, made him heap abuse on Edgar, emphasized by a furious pounding on the black walnut table. The young lady suffering from an overproduction of phlegm, a Miss Turner, of Boston, fainted dead away, while the gentleman who looked like Burnside pulled his whiskers and, upsetting the chair, ran out of the house, never to return. An obscurity in this life, there was no one to spare a word for me in the next.

Have you ever attended a séance, Moran?

Well, one doesn't need tricks and hocus-pocus to conjure. During the months I spent in Poe's company, I sometimes felt the unseen presences inhabiting this world, as you might an electric current in Faraday's induction ring. You thrill to a spark of something vital and alarming when you read the stories. I also sense it when I stand before Eakins's big canvas and see myself engulfed by a turbid atmosphere of paint. I suppose it's the macabre, which Eakins's picture and Poe's work share—in my opinion— that connects them, no matter how divergent their art and personalities. One feels dismay . . . terror—*I* feel reason overthrown by pigment and oil. By words scattered on a page. I'm amazed how skillful writers have the power to create worlds, invoke the dead, make phantoms and figments that persuade us, apparently without effort, of their materiality. I'm a doctor; my art is practical, not magical. I make nothing new; I repair what's been broken or decayed. I cannot make life out of nothing or raise the dead. I mend, Moran, like any seamstress.

Help yourself to the whiskey. No doubt you think me a poor storyteller to take so long to begin. But I like to let the thread unspool slowly, taking its own time and finding its own end. I like to take my time over a meal, a glass, a pipeful of tobacco, a tale. I'd like to hear yours, Moran, if only there were time. But you have a general waiting for you in Philadelphia, and generals cannot be kept waiting by their subalterns. Will you go west again and fight the Indians?

I don't envy you. Custer is a vainglorious man, self-serving and callous.

Have you ever seen a likeness of Edward Hicks's painting *The Peaceable Kingdom*? There the wolf does lie down with the lamb, and the leopard with the kid. There and nowhere else on earth. Poe once said to me, "The turmoil in men's souls is the prelude to a universal catastrophe. Beside ourselves with fear, we claw at one another and, unsated, gnaw at our own vitals." If you want to know humankind at its worst, read Edgar Poe. For virtue, read Whitman.

You said that Whitman visited you during the war, in the hospital at Washington City.

I'm glad you haven't forgotten him, Moran. He's a kind, compassionate man. A great and mighty heart has Whitman. He's dying of it, you know. Oh, it was a stroke that turned that robust, lusty man into an invalid, but to me it is his compassionate heart that is coming asunder. One can die of an excess of love, just as readily as one can perish of misanthropy, as was the case with Poe. By the time you get back from the Badlands, if you do, you may not find Walt Whitman still among the living. But if any soul can persist after the body's death, his can.

I said that the soul is a kind of organ, although I never saw it when I had to lay bare men's innards in field hospitals. Scenes of the slaughterhouse are common when our kind bares its fangs. You might expect to see the soul gleam along a scalpel's edge, like a light trembling in anticipation of extinction. I saw it dead in the heaps of amputated limbs, the shattered bones, the stony eyes, the bright unfurling of intestines—caught death's sharp scent from pails of blood and excrement, the putrefaction of gangrene. But I don't need to tell you, Moran: You lost an eye to the soul's disease. It was venomous in those days, when we were visited by a plague of enmity. How else can we explain Shiloh, Antietam, Stones River, Gettysburg, Andersonville but as a sickness to which few might claim immunity? The death of a man or woman is no more than a rehearsal for Armageddon, which will come, Moran, if not in our own time, then in a future too terrible to imagine. Maybe the soul has always been as Poe disclosed its baleful influence in his tales and in the perturbations of his characters.

I was an army surgeon, a student of Dr. Thomas Dent Mütter's, a friend to Edgar Poe, who made me a character in his nightmares. How could I be otherwise than a pessimist?

Poe was not the wicked man Griswold claimed in his scurrilous biography. I remember his obituary on Poe's death, published in the *New York Tribune*: "Edgar Allan Poe is dead. He died in Baltimore the day before yesterday. This announcement will startle many, but few will be grieved by it."

I grieved, Moran, and I had every reason not to. And if I no longer read his stories, it's only that I'm afraid to lose myself in them once more. One can, you know, when gazing into a mirror.

Philadelphia, January 1844

I met the man whom I would later know to be Edgar Allan Poe at Jefferson Medical College in Philadelphia, where I was employed in Dr. Mütter's laboratory. At the time, I was living with my mother and brother in a small house in Northern Liberties, one of the city's river wards. My father had died some years before, when I was seven or eight years old. He'd been a hand in one of the mills along the Delaware and died, I would guess, of sarcoidosis or some other disease of the lungs. I remember his cough, the deep cuts on his hands, the cotton lint in his hair. Of his death, I recall the gaunt body laid out in a coffin set on trestles in the front room of our house. I can still see the undertaker's hearse, the mournful ride to Palmer Cemetery over Frankford Road's loaf-shaped cobbles, an iron gate, the raw earth, black and sodden with December rain, the steamy breath of the mourners, the wet clay thudding onto my father's wooden box, my mother's face hidden by a heavy veil—properties of a melodrama or a gothic tale. A superb needlewoman, she sewed fancy clothes for rich ladies. Franklin, my elder brother, worked as a stevedore on the coal wharves. I was a grocer's boy. Our means may have been straitened, but, thankfully, we were not destitute. By renting the back room to a German cigar maker, we could keep our little house on Oak Street.

At seventeen, I was hired as a porter at the medical college. The following year, I was made custodian of Dr. Mütter's medical curiosities. I'd been to school and could read; I was likable, willing, and, fortunately, a not overly sensitive young man. There was little in that hospital that could turn my stomach. Dr. Mütter collected oddities and freaks of nature: dried tissue, skeletal remains where the initiated could "read the bones" for illness and trauma, waxed models of hideous deformities, body parts, cysts, tumors, kidney and gallstones, brains, embryos—all put up in jars, in alcohol, as if they were your mother's brandied peach preserves. I was so often among those ghastly remnants of suffering that, during the last war when I sawed off a man's leg for the first time or sewed up a shrapnel-riddled bowel, my iron constitution was proof against squeamishness.

"You have an admirable tolerance for the products of misery," Dr. Mütter once said to me. He had passed a reeking dish of some yellowish matter under my nose and had insisted that I smell it. I snuffled and, despite its noxiousness, did not reveal to him my disgust. He would often test my resolve in this highly empirical manner. "The pathologist can sometimes diagnose a disease by its stench," he said. "The Chinese physician will adjust the body's humors according to the odor of the stool. We can learn much from Oriental medicine."

I admit to a fascination verging on the morbid for Mütter's pickled monstrosities, which P. T. Barnum would have coveted for his American Museum. I've often wondered what it might signify about me as a man, apart from the physician I am, to have been drawn to what the world calls horror. When I dusted the specimen jars, polished the oak cabinets, and rid the glass cases of the fingerprints of the curious, I would thrill at the varieties of abnormality that nature, in her capriciousness, had produced.

There's a curiosity, Moran, comprised of pity, of joy in having been spared nature's enormities, and of a perverse thrill of disgust, that causes us to gaze in fascination at the ugly. The beautiful can preen themselves in it, while we others can smile at ideal Beauty's overthrow. I've always thought it strange that Edgar Poe, who valued beauty and good taste above all other aesthetic qualities, should have found the horrific attractive. He was like a physician charting the course of a grave illness. He was obsessed by the pathology of the human soul, which he could not cure. But his record of its disease is a masterpiece of elegance, reason, and intuition worthy of his own detective, M. Dupin.

"Read this book, Edward," said Mütter, handing me a much-used copy of *Elements of Pathological Anatomy*, which had been published a few years before. It was written by Samuel Gross.

Yes, Moran, the same Dr. Gross painted by Thomas Eakins in '75. He replaced Mütter when he resigned because of ill health. My years have taught me not to be surprised by the apparently happenstance needlework that stitches the fabric of the universe together. In time, its pattern will become evident. Edgar wrote, "And (strange, oh strangest mystery of all!) I found, in the commonest objects of the universe, a circle of analogies."

Dr. Mütter was pleased with the interest I showed in his collection and, later, put me to work in the surgery, where I would clean up after an operation and carry pails of diseased tissue, bone, and bloody bandages to the incinerator. The good man would one day surprise me by paying my tuition to attend the medical school—class of 1853. In time, I became his protégé, taking notes during surgery, seeing to the instruments, and, later, administering diethyl ether or nitrous oxide under his direction. I'm very much in his debt, although I sometimes wish I had chosen another profession. The practice of medicine is gratifying for those who cherish a high opinion of themselves. But beyond the vainglory, there's a danger of overly valuing one's skill, of becoming too self-assured in the presence of life. Edgar, to the contrary, seemed at home in its absence.

What I mean by life, Moran, is the fuse lit by the Creator and snuffed out by Death. The best of us can alleviate suffering and sometimes extend life, but we cannot hope to understand it, no matter how many corpses we pick apart. I saw too many during the war to think otherwise. They soured my sense of a priestly vocation, to which I'd been called, with the vinegar of pessimism. If I'd not been an army surgeon, if I'd not performed so many amputations in the field and lost so many men at the moment of their Calvary, who knows but I might have been cheerful.

In 1844, I had not yet drained the bitter cup. I was a frank and friendly young man. I endeared myself to Dr. Mütter, who was esteemed by his patients as much for his genial manner as for his surgical finesse. My God, the man's hands were a blur during an operation, astounding his students and peers alike! Ambidextrous, he could work twice as fast as any other Jefferson surgeon, perhaps any other practitioner in the city. I vividly recall the operation to reconstruct Nathaniel Dickey's monstrous facial deformity: The instruments flashed under the gaslights as the unfortunate young man endured twenty-five minutes of scarcely imaginable agony, sitting in a chair, with nothing to mitigate the pain except for Mütter's calm, gentle eyes to fix his own upon. That surgery was the closest thing to a miracle I've ever seen. Equally transfixed, Poe was sitting in the visitors' gallery. When Mütter held up a shaving mirror and Nathaniel smiled for the first time in his life to see a human face reflected there, Poe exclaimed, "Eureka!"

I was one of Dr. Mütter's assistants when I first laid eyes on Edgar Poe, although I didn't know his name then. Mütter was too intent on showing off his specimens to think of introducing me. And so, having finished my catalogue notation on the skull of a bargeman with a large, high cranial vault, who'd died of cerebral apoplexy, I left them to themselves. I'd only glanced at Poe, but I was struck by a hectic light in his eyes. Moreover, I had the impression that his face, which later I thought handsome, was at that moment warped as if by a gigantic strain. I'd seen such faces and such eyes before, in patients strapped to the table when Mütter lifted one of his shining instruments from the crimson plush, like a priest offering the chalice to the Almighty.

Later that afternoon, while I was pickling a liver recently taken from a carpenter dead of cirrhosis, Mütter entered with a pleased expression. He had changed his waistcoat and stock—dandyism was his only folly. For all his fastidiousness, he was not an egotist. He was cultured and urbane and, like Poe, absorbed in problems of aesthetics—in his case, those of the human body. He understood that a disfigured face can cause suffering every bit as keenly felt by the patient as a disease of the organs or corruption of the blood. He brought home to America the innovations in reparative and reconstructive surgery he'd learned in Paris.

"Do you know who that gentleman was, Edward?" Dr. Mütter asked, rubbing his hands in satisfaction.

"No, sir, I can't say that I do."

I was used to the sight of odd gentlemen ogling the exhibits.

"Edgar Poe." I must have given him a blank look, for he went on impatiently. "Haven't you ever read one of his tales? 'William Wilson' . . . 'The Gold-Bug' . . . 'The Murders in the Rue Morgue.' He is our most celebrated author of the macabre; there's nothing to match him for the horrific effect rendered in the most accomplished style. His fame had already jumped the Atlantic when I was studying in Paris. You must get hold of his work, Edward. If I think of it tonight, I'll bring you my copy of Lowell's magazine, *The Pioneer.* It contains Poe's excellent story, 'The Tell-Tale Heart.'"

"Thank you, Dr. Mütter, I'd like that."

"You'll have a chance to see him for yourself. He's fascinated by our collection. It was the reason for his visit today. He said he would like very much to return, and I agreed he should. You'll give him every assistance when he does visit us again, Edward."

"I'll be happy to do what I can, Dr. Mütter."

THE FOLLOWING WEEK, Poe did return, and I escorted him amid the cabinets, answering his many questions. He, too, was someone whose stomach could not be easily turned. His dark eyes were bright, but without the flashing intensity I had seen in them on his first visit. His black sack coat and hat were shabby, if carefully brushed. He appeared to be a gentleman who had suffered a reversal of fortune. A man of less than average height, he nonetheless carried himself with the dignity of the sergeant major and, later, the West Point cadet he had been in his youth. He was only thirty-five when I knew him, but his youth was already far behind him. He looked used up. He'd been living with Virginia and Mrs. Clemm, his aunt and mother-in-law, in poverty that can only be described as abject, and, in five years' time, he would die of it. The *Baltimore Clipper* would report his demise, in that city, as the result of "congestion of the brain." But it was poverty that killed him, Moran, and not insanity, opium, or drink, as his critics proclaimed and the world has been happy to believe. Ordinary people relish a scandal and delight in the fall of those greater than themselves.

Poe could be, at times, a drunkard and an abuser of ether and laudanum. I doubt any man in his circumstances and with his nervous temperament—he was an uncommonly nervous man—could have behaved otherwise. During the months I knew him, I took ether and laudanum and soused myself with rum and gin. Happily for me, my temperament does not favor addiction; I seldom drink now and use laudanum only for toothache. In truth, I sometimes stood at the brink with Poe, although I was sensible of the danger and drew back in time.

Did he find the view beautiful? Did he find life as it is lived by the majority of us deadening?

Yes.

Edgar saw a strange beauty in suffering. His imagination thrilled to the burlesque of existence. He seldom smiled when I knew him. I've seen the daguerreotype called "Annie," taken in his final year. His face shows the gigantic strain I mentioned, as though it were about to come asunder. He's cockeyed in the picture—the right orb oddly swiveled. His thin lips come together in a grimace. One sees such faces in the asylum. But I tell you, Moran, he was *not* mad—not when he set pen to paper. A madman could not have written as he did. Nor could a dope fiend or a chronic alcoholic. His faculties were concentrated, his mind clear, his hand steady.

Once, I saw it for myself, Moran: how he wrote—with what extraordinary application. He believed me to be asleep in a chair in the corner of his room. Bent over the foolscap, his hand seemed a thing apart, so still he was except for it. The fingertips of its fellow rested on his forehead—that lofty brow signifying ratiocination, imagination, determination, all of which a mind at the acme of possibility is capable. He was someone rare and untrammeled by convention. Like a man with a rope and pulley, he could raise himself *above* himself. He had the gift to stand outside of the little empire given us at birth and see it clearly. Anyone else would have gone insane, but I tell you, Poe did not! It was I who did. For a time, I was at my wit's end, in thrall to Edgar's magnetic personality.

That was thirty years ago and more; Poe's been dead for over a quarter of a century. I'm a careful observer of the body's minutest motions, its fevers, crises, maladies, disturbances, but however clearly I seem to see my past, I can't be certain that what I remember of it is the truth. Memory is as liable to blight as the soul, both of which survive the departed—the one, in fame or infamy, the other in eternity, if there's such a thing. As a surgeon and an unconvinced Christian, I tend to doubt it.

To be honest, Moran, I don't believe in the immortal soul or in God's heaven, except as a solace against the terror at midnight. Next to annihilation, Poe's horrors are only whimsies. No, I've poked about in too many innards. If the soul were there to be seen, I ought to have seen it—at least some evidence of its having been, as the scorch mark evinces the quenched flame. Even after my three months with Poe, I find it hard to accept the immaterial realm—or, perhaps, my skepticism is the result of the time I spent with him. What cannot be seen smacks too much of his fancies, which I detest. The supernatural, the supersensual, is what I also find objectionable in Eakins's picture: the intimation of a world beyond the senses, at the end of the tunnel and in the painted murk of the spectators. If I would open the palm of my hand with a knife, I'd see the actuality of what lies hidden from view.

At nineteen, I might have believed myself to be Poe's disciple and apprentice, but I doubt I was ever truly suited to the role. Even now, I accept the bituminous quality of the world—unmalleable, black, flammable—but I don't cultivate despair or find it seductive. No, I prefer the light of day to darkness, the music of Mozart to Bach, a comical story of Mark Twain to a somber one by Hawthorne, Melville, or by Edgar Poe. This is, however, to be my story of the winter months I spent with him. And I swear to you, Moran, I will tell it, if not straight out—I can't help meandering—then truly—if the truth can be known and told with so insufficient a means as words. I ought to have been a dauber. I'd like to spend the rest of my days painting luminous landscapes like Bierstadt's *Among the Sierra Nevada* and Thomas Cole's

The Oxbow. I'd leave hellish scenes to the gloomy apostles of Hieronymus Bosch or the German Dürer.

ON HIS THIRD VISIT to "Mütter's museum," as the students called it, Poe asked to see the catalogue of skulls. He was dressed exactly as he'd been on his previous visits and as he would be when he watched Nathaniel Dickey's transfiguration and shouted his "Eureka!"—which, later, he'd retract. Despite the threadbare condition of his clothes, Edgar was always immaculately groomed. That day, I had the opportunity to study him. His sunken eyes might have persuaded me that the irises were black, had I not seen clearly that they were gray and flecked with tiny amber lights. The chestnut hair curled to the point of unruliness, but, except for a scraggly mustache, his face was cleanly shaved. His chin was classically molded, the face a pale oval, the brow imposing, lofty, intelligent. The physiognomists have made much of Poe's high forehead.

Do you believe that our qualities—our souls, if you like the word—can be read, like Braille, in the bumps on top of our heads? Aren't you convinced that the countenance betrays character, its quirks, inclinations, passions, humors, and that the shape of the cranial skull determines our mental faculties?

No? Then you're an enlightened man; the sciences of physiognomy and phrenology, refined in the last century by Franz-Josef Gall, are only now being questioned. In 1844, we believed in the Austrian anatomist's mapping of the brain according to its functions, and in Lavater's insistence that outer appearance reveals inner character. Poe took it as a matter of course. He'd read *Physiognomische Fragmente zur Beförderung der Menschenkenntnis und Menschenliebe* and Sir Thomas Browne's treatises. Poe's tale—the one I stole from him and in whose composition I was intimately involved—had everything to do with those doubtful sciences. He spoke of them at the college, after I had taken the catalogue from the shelf and laid open its pages to his devouring eye. He was sitting at a large table, whose polished oak shone in the sun of a mild January afternoon. His nicely shaped hands fluttered eagerly and then settled on the folio pages crowded with script and illustrations done in India ink.

"Mr. Poe," I said, having taken a backward step or two in respect for his privacy.

"Thank you, young man," he said kindly. "Did you make these entries?"

"I did, sir."

"You have a fine hand, almost feminine in its graces."

His manner was genial, even courtly. I was surprised to be the object of a gentleman's goodwill. He *was* a gentleman, Moran; he would've been one had he been dressed in rags.

"Before I ever went to school, my mother had taught me to make my letters."

"One can read something of a man in his penmanship. Something secret and otherwise hidden. Jacob Böhme believed in the doctrine of signatures, meaning God marked the things of this world with signs indicating their purpose. Do you think he was right—what is your name?"

"Edward Fenzil."

"A good German name."

"My father came here from Bavaria."

"I never knew mine, or my mother, either. So, Edward, do you believe that the human face bears the warrants of its personality?"

"Yes, Mr. Poe, I do."

"Charles Dickens's characters—you are acquainted with Mr. Dickens's stories?"

"I read *Oliver Twist*."

"Fagin, Bill Sikes, Nancy, Mr. Brownlow—their faces are an index to their souls."

"What do you see when you look at mine?" I asked him.

I knew it was an audacious question; Poe might have bridled at my familiarity on such slight acquaintance. But he had shown me unusual courtesy; moreover, I saw in *his* face, which was a puzzling mixture of the beautiful and strange, not the slightest reluctance or ill will. If anything, he appeared perfectly willing to accept me—boy that I was—as a person worthy of his consideration. Whether he was at heart comprehensive in his affections, like Walt Whitman, or exclusive, I don't know. But that winter the two of us hobnobbed with men and women the world finds objectionable, even depraved, and he never carped or raised an eyebrow in disdain.

He gazed at my face awhile. He went so far as to follow its features with his fingertips and then feel with them the contours hidden beneath my hair. As he looked at me, I studied his eyes, lively and lambent with curiosity. The gray irises appeared to darken, assuming an almost violet tint difficult to describe. Their effect on me was magnetic:

He held my eyes with his own, which did now seem black as pitch. I grew uncomfortable under his gaze but could not look away—did not wish to. I felt—I was too absorbed by his will to say that I "thought"—I was drowning—no, not drowning, buried. Entombed. It was nonsense. I had imagined it all. His eyes were not on mine; they were roving the landscape of my face. Poe was no mesmerist. He was, I saw after I had broken my fixed stare, a prepossessing man, slender, compact, amiable. A man of unusual gifts, who would soon befriend me.

"I am a poet," he said, apropos of nothing.

"I've read two of your stories."

"Not my poems?" When I shook my head, he seemed disappointed. "Well, Edward, your face is a good one, and I see in it a pleasing nature and an intelligence above the ordinary."

"I'm glad to hear it, sir."

His expression suddenly altered as grasslands will when a cloud moves against the sun.

"Is something the matter, Mr. Poe?"

"There was something, Edward. . . ."

"What is it?"

"On your temple, immediately above the right ear, I felt a pronounced inclination toward destructiveness. Mind you, phrenology reveals only propensity, not necessity. I imagine most men's skulls would tell a similar tale. Women's, too, for what I've known of some of them."

To this day, I don't know if he was amusing himself with me or if those traits were really stamped upon my face and skull. In time, I'd have proof of Lavater's doctrine to make me wish I'd never met Edgar Poe: proof that outward appearance and the heart's secret places are bound by filaments as unbreakable as the cables of the Brooklyn Bridge.

"Never mind, Edward. These 'sciences' may be only a fantasy indulged in by novelists and mountebanks. Let us see what story the catalogue has to tell," he said, glancing at its pages. "And bring me the skulls to which these notes refer, if you please."

I fetched eight of what Hamlet had pondered in the graveyard at Elsinore. All in a row, they made a ghastly totem. To unearth a single skull is a surprise; to ponder a heap of them, a shock. It is the same with all things macabre.

"Thank you, Edward."

I stood slightly behind him and watched as he contemplated each skull in light of its ledger entry. He caressed the polished bone like a blind person taking the measure of another's face. His touch was full of tenderness. He might have been stroking his beloved or the death mask of a man he'd venerated. The sun, which had strengthened as it escaped the net of bare poplar trees across the street, made the memento mori gleam eerily. Although I had often held them in my hands, I shivered. Looking back on those days, I realize there was in Poe a *vital connection* with death. There's sense in the oxymoron: He was never so alive as when he mused on extinction. I couldn't have said then which entranced him more: his subject matter or his art. Now I know they were indivisible.

Having surveyed the skulls, he read their sordid particulars in a voice usually reserved for memorials to the honored dead. I thrilled at each fatal entry like a boy stirred by a martial air.

Name, age: Unknown
Gender: Female
Place of Origin: Unknown
Cause of Death: Suicide
Description: Metopic suture, nasal crest, low cranial
    vault

Name, age: Thorvald Becker, 51
Gender: Male
Place of Origin: Saxony
Cause of Death: Cut his throat because of extreme
    poverty
Description: Catholic. Frontal grooves, multiple
    supraorbital foramina

Name, age: Adrao Rabi, 40
Gender: Male
Place of Origin: Galicia
Cause of Death: Died of trauma in the Charity
    Hospital
Description: Railway worker. Continuous brow ridge

Name, age: Mirjam Dekker, 46
Gender: Female
Place of Origin: Holland
Cause of Death: Phlebitis, complicated fracture of
    the femur
Description: Prominent brow ridge, rhomboid orbits

Name, age: Czeslaw Vogel, 26
Gender: Male
Place of Origin: Warsaw
Cause of Death: Hanged
Description: Murderer. Dental pathology (possible
   abscesses)

Name, age: Menno Kira, 24
Gender: Male
Place of Origin: Friesland
Cause of Death: Gunshot wounds
Description: Sailor

Name, age: Nada Sokić, 17
Gender: Female
Place of Origin: Croatia
Cause of Death: Smallpox
Description: Mill hand. Tooth edges straight and
   continuous

Name, age: Biktop Shamo, unknown
Gender: Male
Place of Origin: Krasnoe, Ukraine
Cause of Death: Self-inflicted removal of testicles
Description: Member of Russian sect believing in
   castration. Dual left supraorbital foramina

From time to time, he would address a question over his
shoulder to where I stood leaning over his. I had to clar-
ify the anatomical descriptions and show him the places
on the skulls to which they referred. He was amazed by

the violent deaths that many of their former "owners" had suffered.

"More likely than not such men and women as these used to be were left with no one to mourn them," he said thoughtfully. "If any did grieve, I imagine they would have done so alone, like an animal crawling off into the bushes to give birth or to die."

I nodded and, despite my affectation of nonchalance, I felt the corners of my mouth turn down. I was nineteen, remember, and, though my family's means were meager, we were happy, and I had yet to have my optimism blighted. It would take a winter with Poe, the hell he opened up to me, and, much later, a war to make me sullen and afraid. I smiled and assumed a cheerful countenance, determined to ingratiate myself. Why I should have cared, I don't know, unless it was his eyes—what I saw in them: a depth of knowledge or, rather, of experience far beyond me and the confines of my life, no matter how I might have been surrounded by monstrosities, sickness, and death.

"Those with none to claim them end up in the almshouse cemetery or, if they're lucky, here, in Dr. Mütter's 'cabinet of horrors'—begging your pardon, Mr. Poe."

I winked drolly and would have done a comic gig suitable for the music hall to gain his favor. I must have appeared ridiculous, but I was determined that he should see me as a plucky lad uncowed by my gruesome occupation or his celebrity.

"Why should they be lucky?"

I wondered if he would reprove me for my nerve but went on just the same. "It's more pleasant for their mortal remains to spend the next life, such as it may be, in the warmth and light. I hate to think of myself put into the ground, with no other company than beetles and worms."

Poe was amused, so I continued to jolly him.

"Anyone would be glad to have his leftovers cleaned and dusted regularly by a smart young man like me. And isn't it a privilege for them to advance the cause of science when, more than likely, these skulls did nothing in life but think where their next drink was coming from?"

"You are a scoundrel, Mr. Fenzil."

"Thank you, sir," I said, bowing. "I value your good opinion."

Composing himself, he returned to his cranial examination. I, in turn, examined him further. The curls of his hair fell romantically over a frayed high collar. His shoulders were narrow, but I'd been mistaken in my first impression: Poe was not delicate, although many of his lady admirers thought him so. In his slender, erect frame, there was vigor, a strength of sinew consonant with tenacity and grit. He'd been a soldier, and, impoverished, he lived much of his mature life among ruffians and hard men. He knew how to get on with all sorts. During the winter of '44, we visited low haunts and did things good Christians would have seen us jailed for, if not hanged. But I had the feeling that he did what he did for the sake of his art and not for any relish of vice. He wasn't vicious. He might have been weak—his troubles made him so— but he was not the moral degenerate some people say, no more than Dr. Mütter was for doting on nature's freaks.

"Even now, after boiling and bleaching, this skull

has secrets it won't tell," said Poe while he held Mirjam Dekker's mortal portion in his hands and peered into the empty eye sockets.

"It has nothing anymore to tell them with," I said flippantly.

"The truth will out, regardless." He put the bone down on the table. "In its shape, it is as ancient as the mountains and, like them, keeps the time of the firmament and of the first atom."

Poe had a conscience; he wrote about its crises—and something more: the dread that slowly erodes the better part of us with the inevitability of water dripping on a rock. Who of us can stand between the pit and the pendulum and not give way? I believe that this was the human tragedy that fascinated him—not evil, but the faulty center, the rot in the roof beam, the crack in the keystone, an almost inevitable flaw at the heart of every human character, made to beat in a "story" that is not of its making and not entirely within its control. This is the awful truth that Edgar Poe realized, what he labored under, what he wrote about, and what the poor man died of. Not alcohol, brain congestion, opiates, consumption, cholera, rabies, or suicide did him in, but his embattled senses and embittered virtue, together with a lack of means and prospects. He was Micawber without optimism. I knew Edgar Allan Poe for only a short time; I was a principal character in one of his horrors.

I no longer blame him. I was too impressionable, too ready to fall under his spell, his dark enchantment, too young, too inexperienced to resist. I tell you, Moran, I lost myself that winter! Now, each morning, I look at my face in the shaving mirror to assure myself that I am still here. I and my unsavory—you are kind to take no notice of it.

Peering in a mirror is the nearest most children come to magic, or madness; for them, the looking glass alters, if only slightly, the world submerged in its depths. The boy in my mother's cheval glass, staring at me with quizzical, even frightened, eyes was not me. I had momentarily lost myself in it! Each time, I would come away feeling diminished and afraid. And yet, I would return to stand and look—helpless to do otherwise—as I do now at Eakins's picture.

When does the last ferry to Philadelphia leave?

Six o'clock tonight. Will that give you enough time to meet your General Custer?

Fine! I'm glad you don't find me tedious. Not yet anyway. You wouldn't be the first to sit and squirm! But I like to reflect, as I go, because for me a tale's use and interest lie exactly in the notions that come to mind as the narrative unspools. Try some of my tobacco, won't you? Virginia spiced with perique. I bought it in New York the last time I visited Bellevue Hospital. I was there to see the marvelous job Dr. Smith's doing for the insane.

"This Vogel who was hanged . . ." said Poe, stabbing at the catalogue entry with a finger, like a man stubbing out a cigarette. "I'd like to have been a thought inside his skull the moment the hangman dropped him. Time must have been in suspension during the body's dying fall to the end of the rope and the snap of the neck. I've a feeling he had space enough to think with an intensity, a clarity, a rationality he'd never known before. Edward, I could write a book about that appalling moment, which was, for him, eternity, if I'd seen and thought what this young man did on his way toward extinction."

A merry notion, Moran! But that was Edgar Poe's way.

"It would be obscene!" I said, honesty momentarily subduing a false humility.

Poe shrugged. "The mind cannot help its thoughts."

It can keep its mouth shut, I said to myself. His fantasy had horrified me.

Poe picked up Vogel's skull and weighed it in his hands as if it were gold. I was struck by his admiration for the thing. He appeared suddenly to have been possessed by— well, I didn't know what he found compelling, unless it was Czeslaw Vogel's ghost, which had been shut up inside his skull like a genie in a lamp. I'd handled it many times, and never once had it incited in me anything other than a vague sympathy. To be honest, it was more my curiosity that would move me. Vogel meant nothing to me. Edgar's curiosity was plain to see as he looked at what had been the face of a young man from Poland, who had come to grief in the Kensington ward of Philadelphia and had met his end on the penitentiary gibbet.

"His teeth were bad," said Poe, running his finger over the dead man's molars. "'Possible abscesses,' you've written here."

"That's right," I said, leaning over his shoulder to read the annotation penned in my own fine cursive hand.

"A toothache can drive a person to distraction until there's nothing in the world except the pain of it."

I grunted in assent, remembering how I'd suffered from a carious incisor that not even oil of clove could calm. I felt the gap left by its extraction with the tip of my tongue and shuddered at the memory.

"An abscess is worse. Perhaps it was an agony too great to be borne," Poe said as much to himself as to me. "For Vogel. Pain is not absolute: Each of us tolerates it as he can." Poe tapped at a diseased tooth. "There is no telling what a mouth such as this could have done to his mind." He was silent a moment. "What do you think, Edward? Could a man's mouth turn him into a murderer? I can imagine killing even a wife if she was foolish enough to nag and vex a man while he was in the throes of a toothache."

I had no answer for him.

"I put it to you, Edward: Is the good man's goodness fixed and impossible to pervert—an unswerving moral compass? Or can it be turned aside by pain?"

He expected an answer, and I gave him one: "I suppose if the pain is great and the moral nature weak . . ."

"You're being evasive, my friend. But let it go, for now." He fell to studying Vogel's skull again. "The body is not the only seat of pain. The mind, too, Edward—the mind can know pain more terrible than the body's. Or have you never in your young life suffered doubt, envy, jealousy, bereavement, fear, desire, shame? I have. They have teeth, those emotions, and they gnaw and rend."

I was beginning to regret that Dr. Mütter had charged me with satisfying Poe's interest, which I found increasingly alarming. By now, I'd read "Ligeia" and "William Wilson," besides "The Tell-Tale Heart." I understood and even enjoyed Poe's frightening inventions. But to see one taking shape before my eyes was quite another thing. I knew that a literary creation might scare the daylights out of me but that it could not harm me. I sensed, however, that what Poe, by his uncanny gifts, had been empowered to invoke was dangerous. All at once, I wanted to escape his influence and thought that if he were once more to catch my eye, I would be lost—an idea as far-fetched as his own crotchets. I let my eyes rest a moment on his alpaca coat, whose shoulder seam was in need of a needle and thread. Foolishly, I prayed that he would not turn around. I would be safe for as long as I did not see his face, nor he mine.

I think that the dread I felt had been encouraged by the residue of the tales of his I had read, by the skulls and pathological exhibits surrounding me, and by the sudden obscurity into which the room was plunged. The low sun was hidden by a shoal of clouds, and the gaslights had yet to be lit. I reminded myself that the person who sat in front of me, poring over the cranial souvenir of Czeslaw Vogel, was only a poor scribbler dressed in a shabby suit of clothes. He may have been a gentleman, a graduate of a fine university, and a former West Point cadet, but, as docent of Mütter's freak show, I earned enough money to buy a chesterfield coat, a shawl-collared vest, a fancy cravat, and leather gaiters. While not turned out so elegantly as Dr. Mütter, I was a fashion plate next to this broken-down scribe.

"If only it could talk!" cried Poe, musing on the Polish skull. "What a tale it would have to tell! It would outdo anything my mortal imagination could contrive, and I'd gladly be its amanuensis if only it would speak its mind. Think of it, Edward! It could betray the secrets of the grave. What wouldn't I give if poor Yorick here could only work the hinges of its jaw and speak! I'd make a Faustian bargain to gain the knowledge locked within this bone."

He knocked absurdly on the skull like a man impatient for a door to open. His eyes glazed over. He appeared to be in the grasp of something beyond reach of ordinary mortals.

"Time is slowing," he said in a leaden voice. "Each moment grows and fattens like a drop of rain on a window sash, waiting to fall."

His words were wild, and I trembled to hear them. And then he placed the skull upon the table and began to run his fingers over it, as though he meant to read Vogel's character in the fleshless face.

"Edward, I can almost see the man himself, as he used to be."

In spite of myself, I found myself drawing nearer. I watched Poe's shapely fingers caress what was left of Vogel. The room grew darker, a dog barked outside in the distance, and a door in a remote corridor of the hospital closed audibly. I might have stepped into a gothic novel or one of Poe's own literary horrors. I was deliciously frightened and enthralled.

"He was miserably poor," said Poe, his fingertips in motion around the contours of the skull. I noticed that his eyes were shut, the lashes long and dark. A handsome man, I thought, now that I see him clearly, if a strangely fashioned one. "An intelligent man, who spoke English poorly and must, of necessity, take menial jobs that were beneath him and that he resented. A sad and lonely person, driven by demons and want to murder—a girl, perchance, who had spurned him, or a man, an overseer, who had insulted him. And so he was hanged."

With his slender fingers, Poe encircled the place where, in life, Vogel's throat had been. "I feel the rope around my neck." With a finger, Poe circled the empty sockets of bone, first the right, then the left. "Here, where his eyes used to be, I see the executioner, an inmate standing behind a barred window overlooking the gray stones of the prison yard, the gallows, a bird, a cloud, a patch of jimsonweed, a newspaper tucked under the warden's arm, the shadow under the chaplain's lean jaw, the slow ascent of a poplar tree as I float from the scaffold down toward an earth that I will never walk upon again and in which I will never rest. Instead of a grave, I am fated to spend the afterlife here, on a shelf—the godlike part of me that used to think."

I found myself wondering if, by a rare sympathy, Poe had not provoked Vogel's ghost to speak, so cunningly had he thrown his voice into the skull. He fell into a reverie, and in the abruptly restored silence, I heard myself cough to break the eerie spell.

"A pretty figment, eh?" he said. "I might work it up into a story."

"You're as good a ventriloquist as Harrington, who played the Chestnut last year."

"It is your imagination that makes it seem so. Nevertheless, I thank you."

He stood and wound his muffler around his neck. "I'll leave you now to your mute and shameless admirers. Virginia will have my supper waiting. You must come to our house on North Seventh, Edward. Sissie will be very pleased to meet you."

"Thank you, Mr. Poe. I will."

WHEN I FIRST MET VIRGINIA, whom Poe called "Sis" or "Sissie," she was a pretty, dark woman of twenty-two, whose porcelain complexion was beginning to show the warrants of consumption. Nearer my own age than Edgar's, she had been thirteen when they married; he, twenty-six. They were first cousins. Consanguinity may have made them shy. They adored each other, exchanged tender words in my presence, but never, during my visits to their house that winter, did I see them betray, by so much as a glance, the amorousness evident in even a modest young husband and wife who are in conjugal matters of one accord. I don't believe they ever redeemed their pledges with their bodies, however twined their two souls might have been. Whether the fault, if fault it was, lay with her or with him or had been by tacit agreement enshrined among their covenants, I don't know. In the beginning of their union, she might have been too young. Now, near its end, she was probably too sick to ruddy the marriage bed. What I mean to say, Moran, is that Virginia died a virgin. This, anyway, is the opinion of those who knew her.

Is it, also, mine?

I know no more of what passed between them than anyone does of the private lives of men and women together. But I would guess that was the case.

Were they happy?

Good Lord, I hope so! They seemed to be that winter. I never believed the rumors.

Ha! So you're not a man who despises scandal and gossip as the staple of idle women and mollycoddles? Well, sir, when, in 1847, she climbed into her death bed, Virginia—I will not call her "Sissie"—claimed with her dying breath that Elizabeth Ellet, one of Edgar's sweethearts—I can't say if they were lovers—had poisoned her. Edgar was not the only person in the Poe household to have been preoccupied with murder. He was a philanderer, if a puerile one: He liked the ladies, and the ladies liked him. But did he bed any of them? Opinion concerning that question is divided.

No, Moran, I'll keep mine to myself.

Sometime later, I saw a likeness of Virginia, rendered after her death, in watercolors, that caught her fragile beauty. I was sorry for her. To have died at twenty-four, even in an age of early death, was a tragedy that, I believe, haunted the pages of Edgar's late prose and poetry and, I'm certain, his mind, which was always overcast by melancholy.

That rainy, cold evening when I visited the Poe house for the first time, Virginia greeted me at the door and led me without ceremony—my boots wet and my coat dripping—to the fire crackling in the grate. She took my coat and hat and gave me one of Edgar's shawls to chase the January chill from my bones. In a moment, he appeared with a smile—I noted the small, even teeth—and a pewter pitcher. He drew the red-hot mulling poker from the fire, and with a merry hiss, orange peel, cinnamon, and clove gave up their aromatic ghosts to the Poes' small candlelit front room. Shortly, I felt the goodness of an excellent rum punch coursing through my veins. I wish I'd some to give you. But I suppose a hard-bitten man like you enjoys his whiskey more.

"Sit down, Edward," said Poe cordially, indicating the

arm chair nearest the fire, whose imps had turned the hearthstone black. "Stretch your legs toward the warmth."

Virginia had disappeared into the kitchen, where Mrs. Clemm, her mother and Poe's aunt, skirmished noisily with a cast-iron pot and a roasting pan, in which four plucked quails lay in state. She was a quiet, capable woman of middle age who had kept house for Edgar and Sissie ever since they'd married. After he'd lost his position at *Graham's Magazine*, the widow became the chief contributor to the household's always slender means. I recall little of the meal. Virginia made only a slight impression on me; she was shy and appeared to be in awe of her husband. Her mother left none at all, beyond a vague recollection of a gingham apron and a ladle with which she spooned pan juices over the roasted birds.

I, too, was in awe of my host, who, that evening, was genial, even jaunty. I'd seldom see him thus, unless he was the worse—or better—for drink or ether. He spoke on diverse subjects: the arrest of Jacob Snively and his Texas freebooters, a pro-slavery mob's attack on Frederick Douglass in Indiana, Charles Dickens's latest installment of *The Adventures of Martin Chuzzlewitt,* and the publication of Poe's own tale "The Gold-Bug" in Philadelphia's *Dollar Newspaper,* for which he received the one-hundred-dollar prize. He would leave Philadelphia for New York City in April, with four dollars and fifty cents in his pocket. I also recall a gaudy parrot, rocking in its cage in a corner of the dining room, squawking "Nevermore." Poe was encouraged by the mimic bird to recite "The Raven" from memory while Mrs. Clemm and I ate plum cake and Virginia raptly attended to her husband's melodramatic recitation.

One line remains with me. "Get thee back into the tempest and the Night's Plutonian shore!" Maybe the rain, which had increased enough to rattle the sashes and submerge the dimly lit room in a tide of shadows, gave the injunction emphasis. The night was magical; we might have been dining in a submarine grotto.

Damn it, Moran, the room wasn't like that! Memory makes it so—addled by time and besotted by Romantic and gothic tales! Ours is the age of the pathological imagination, and I'm as guilty of it as the next man or woman infatuated with the novels of Ann Radcliffe and Clara Reeve. Eighteen hundred and forty-four was a long time ago. I've lived several lives since then. I scarcely recall Poe's little house. It was dark and damp, like most houses—like my own on Oak Street. There was a parrot. The parrot did say "Nevermore." Poe did recite "The Raven," or perhaps he read it. The mulling poker hissed. The rain was noisy on the roof. We talked about the events of the day in the words I've used or some others. I've kept the essence of that winter, here, in my heart, to speak rhetorically. I don't know where the soul would reside, should there turn out to be one after all. Heart or brain or beneath the sternum, which, I suppose, is analogous to the wishbone, although you won't find such a fanciful comparison in Baillie's *The Morbid Anatomy of Some of the Most Important Parts of the Human Body*. But what last wishes might be heard thrilling in the wishbone! What panicky music in that unstrung harp when the last light gleams on the ax's blade—an overture to the dinner gong!

After our dinner, Poe and I sat in the parlor, smoking

cigars and letting the fire weave stories of its own. Our legs were gilded by it. I think we were silent. The hearth fire has a charming influence; it can anesthetize the agitated mind; play a lullaby to quiet jangled nerves. Perhaps I dozed. Thinking back on that night, I experience a sensation of calm; I must have been content. I wonder if I fell asleep, and if I did, was there time enough to dream? And if I'd had a dream, Moran, what might it have been? What phantasms chased each other down the corridors of my sleeping brain? I'd like to remember them. So much that is important gets lost. What a tired old adage that is! Slow and irreversible loss is the quintessence of old age, whose essence is the germ of death implanted at our birth. A doleful thought! But I am speaking of the most doleful of men: Edgar Poe and I.

I roused myself, or he roused me. In any case, he was offering me a tumbler of brandy. He had his in the other hand.

"A color rich as a Virginia copper halfpenny," he said, holding his glass up to the firelight.

I drank mine off at once and felt the pleasant heat against my tongue. I was reminded of the book I'd brought for him and asked to have my coat. Poe called to Virginia, who came from the kitchen with the brandy bottle. Poe was pleased to have his glass filled up again. I declined.

"May I have my coat?" I asked her. "I must be going."

She fetched my coat and stood shyly next to a maple slant-lid desk.

"Dr. Mütter wanted you to have his book in gratitude

for the gift you made him of yours," I said, rooting out the volume from my coat's ample inside pocket.

On his second visit to the college, Poe had given him a morocco-bound copy of *Tales of the Grotesque and Arabesque*, inscribed with the words:

PRESENTED TO THOMAS D. MÜTTER,
WITH RESPECT & GOODWILL,
FROM HIS ADMIRING FELLOW GROTESQUE,
EDGAR A. POE
5TH OF JANUARY 1844

Before I left Poe's house that night, I gave him Dr. Mütter's *Cases of Deformity from Burns, Successfully Treated by Plastic Operations,* which had been published by Merrihew and Thompson, of Philadelphia, the year before. The doctor had returned Poe's compliment with an inscription of his own on the flyleaf:

PRESENTED TO MR. E. A. POE,
IN RECOGNITION OF OUR COMMON MANIA,
THOMAS DENT MÜTTER, M. D.
14TH OF JANUARY 1844

Edgar opened the book to a suite of illustrations showing a woman whose face Mütter had surgically reconstructed after an appalling burn. Her once-pleasant features appeared to have been restored, as if by magic. The medical "wizard" retains the magic wand in the form of a scalpel. I hadn't witnessed the operation, nor had I met the woman, but I'd seen the doctor perform miracles of plastic surgery, an innovation of the school of Paris, where Mütter's native gifts had been given luster. The pages captivated Poe, who sensed in their revelation a story, which he proceeded to sketch for me.

No, on second thought, it was in a barroom on Green Street, near the public landing, several days later, where he wondered aloud about the "meaning" of the woman's transformation.

"Dr. Mütter's book has opened a door through which I never thought to look," said Poe, staring into his glass at the yeasty play of foam.

We had stopped at Kelly's, or O'Shaughnessy's, or O'Malley's—there was no shortage of Irish taprooms in the river wards in those days—to make a poor man's lunch of boiled eggs and beer. I'm embarrassed, still, to recall the superiority I felt toward the patrons there—carters, draymen, and street diggers in rough and dirty clothes—dressed, as I was, à la mode, in a clean linen shirt, standup collar, cravat, and fawn-colored coat. I could be a smug and pompous ass, aping, as I did, Dr. Mütter's stylish dress and demeanor. As you see, Moran, I no longer bother about fashion.

"How's that, Mr. Poe?" I asked, salting my egg.

"Do please call me Edgar."

"What door did you have in mind?"

"Since Sir Thomas Brown, we've known that 'eyes and noses have tongues, and the countenance proclaims the heart and inclinations.' But we could not have supposed, until now, that the proclamation might be revoked; that the wrinkles in that antique writ could be 'ironed out' with a knife and hook, forceps and waxed thread."

I took a bite of hard-boiled egg and chewed.

"Most of us have believed that men's and women's acts are predestined; their fortunes told by bumps on the head and features of the face, bestowed at birth. Phrenology, physiognomy—they're a kind of Presbyterianism of natural philosophy, where predestination makes senseless the idea of freedom of the will. It's a somber thought for those who hope, by education and self-government, to alter the courses of their lives, to improve their stations by hard work and virtue, to exchange the cards dealt them at birth for a better hand. You can dress as elegantly as you please, Edward," he said, undoing my ruby-colored cravat with a flourish, "but you cannot undo the knot fate has tied for you."

I was annoyed by his illustration and knotted up my cravat.

He seemed pleased with himself and, finishing his beer, called for another.

"That was the general idea before 'Mütter's miracle.'"

"I don't know what you're talking about," I said petulantly, tracing an arabesque in the salt that had accumulated on the table.

"The poor woman whose face was changed beyond recognition—her character also must have been altered by the fire. Her features having been transmogrified, her personality could not help but become grotesque. At the very least, she would be shy of people—possibly a recluse—embittered, angry, envious, and jealous of her former self, whom she might have come to detest as someone else, a woman prepossessing and sociable, fortunate and happy."

I nodded to show him I was listening, despite a

distraction in the street, where a man was vomiting onto the cobblestones, to the amusement of two others dressed in leather smocks.

"But Mütter's operation might have restored not only her face but also her personality to what they had been before her accident." His words filled him with excitement.

"I suppose . . ." I said, growing tired of the subject.

"Don't you see, Edward? We aren't necessarily a bounden slave to misfortune. We need not, like the Hindus and the British, resign ourselves to a caste. I'm speaking metaphorically, of course: I view Mütter's procedure as a fable for the *possibility of altering fate itself.* My interest is not in medicine, but in philosophy and literature. What's one woman's face to the overthrow of universal slavery?"

I shuddered for a cause I could not have identified. "The change," I said, "needn't be for the good."

"No." He revolved the glass in his hand and watched the beer roll round the rim. "But there's a story here. . . . Suppose, Edward, that a terrible accident befalls a man— upright, God-fearing, and honorable. His horse bolts, and he's thrown into the street, or else a thief, intent on snatching his wallet, cuts him with a knife. For whatever reason, the man's cheek is scarred . . . disfigured; his once-handsome face ruined. This most excellent of men who had enjoyed the favor of women, the respect of his employer, the esteem of his colleagues, becomes, by the sympathetic reaction of his personality, solitary, irascible, a hateful, villainous person . . . a drunkard or an opium eater. Systematically, he kills his own finer traits and instincts, until, having destroyed himself, having become, as it were, another person, he murders his friend . . . his wife . . . his child."

A man at the table next to ours had leaned toward Edgar while he built his fiction by the addition of one bloody detail on another. For a moment, I thought that the entire barroom had fallen silent under the spell of Poe's rehearsal, but it was only the natural lull in conversation that sometimes follows a lively din. A noise in the street, like a pistol shot, loosened the temporarily stoppered tongues of the handful of patrons remaining in the room. One o'clock had come and gone. The man at the table next to ours laughed oddly, as at a joke whose point you don't quite understand, and returned to his sausage and mash.

"Then, I guess, the murderer, sentenced to death, repents," I said, taking up the broken thread of Poe's anecdote. "His last wish, granted because of his former goodness, is that his disfigurement be repaired by the famous Dr. Mütter, of Jefferson Medical College, so that he might enter heaven in the shape and character of the person he used to be."

"In his Maker's image—yes, yes, Edward. The tale should end so. I thought, when I started to sketch its outline, that it would be so. But my humor is saturnine, my imagination bleak. I part the heavy drapes around the coffin and try to stare down death. And fail—fail to find consolation in this world or the next. I'm temperamentally opposed to redemption—in fiction, that is. The other sort belongs to theology."

The barkeep interposed a damp rag, with which, having taken up our empty plates, he wiped the tabletop. "Another drink, gents?"

"By all means!" replied Edgar grandly.

"None for me," I said, seized by an instant's revulsion caused by the table's unpleasant dampness. "I must be getting back to the 'museum of horrors,' or Mütter will have my liver in one of his jars."

Tossing the damp rag over his shoulder, the barkeep withdrew with our plates and empty glasses. Shortly, he returned with a fresh glass of beer for Edgar. It hissed like a sibyl wishing to reveal a great secret. But it was only the fermentation of hops and yeast I heard.

"You see how easily I'm carried away by my own fancy. It's the curse and blessing of an imaginative mind. To speak frankly, Edward, the world my mind conceives of is more important than that which God made and is everywhere disappointing and absurd. I'm more interested in the truth of fiction than in actuality."

"What's the truth of your tale about the disfigured man?" I asked, laying money on the table to pay for my egg and beer.

"That he murdered, did not repent, was not restored to his former face or self, and was hanged."

"I must be going," I said, pushing back my chair.

"Edward, have you ever seen a hanging?"

"No."

"On the scaffold is where you'll find the truth—not in Mütter's fairy tale. I wish it were otherwise."

THE WORLD MIGHT HAVE ENDED—not in fire, but in snow—so desolate the prison yard appeared below a leaden sky. Snow had fallen during the night; it lay upon the cornices and the window ledges, on the high stone walls and on the gallows' beam. God had damned the curious woman and her man and sentenced us, their heirs to sin and death, to a like inquisitiveness. No sooner had I heard the iron door shut behind me, however, than I wished I hadn't come. What had I to do with the hanging of a stranger? The pickled souvenirs of our kind's brief struggle with death would have been a more welcome sight than the hemp cravat that the condemned man would be wearing to his grave.

By now, I'd read too much of Poe to see the world without an intervening gloom: a gray drizzle of dust or, during this raw January day, an atmosphere composed of icy crystals, biting wind, and dread. I was unmoved when dusting Vogel's skull and, once, to amuse a silly girl, I had kissed his tongueless, gumless, altogether fleshless face. But at the sight of this man—his name was Rudolph Holtz, or Heinz—dragging his misery, like a game leg, up a flight of wooden steps, I trembled. Poe looked on with only a trace of excitement in his gray eyes to leaven an otherwise-impassive expression. He gathered the collar of his shabby coat around his neck, not in an unconscious sympathy for the man who would soon be gathered into eternity, but against the bitter cold.

I was grateful that, for once, Poe had nothing to say; I could not have answered him for the chattering of my teeth. I was scared, Moran. I was familiar with what a man leaves behind after he's departed this life for the next, but the solemn moment of departure—that's a secret better kept untold. My advice to you, Moran, is to avoid a hanging at all costs.

Now Holtz, or Heinz, entered the unearthly suspension

of time that Poe had claimed to experience when he'd pawed over Vogel's skull and imagined in minute detail his own now-concluded transaction with the gallows. Heinz, or Holtz, seemed to mount the rough staircase toward the waiting noose as if he had all the time in the world. I would not have been surprised if winter had been replaced by spring, the gray sky by blue, so very slowly did he mount the wooden treads. With equal slowness, the rope was fitted around his neck, the chaplain muttered "Courage," and the warden nodded toward the executioner, who pulled an iron lever, solemnly, as though to release the bottom of the world itself for humankind to tumble out into extinction. The condemned man descended gravely; I heard a noise like a bowstring when the arrow is let go; he nodded as in farewell to a world that had been unkind, intolerant, or merely indifferent to him. The tautening rope seemed to sting the very air, and then I heard a noise like an arrow's hitting home. I felt the noose tighten. The dead man twisted on his axis. Silence flooded the prison yard, cold and barren as the moon. It seemed to me that even the wind was holding its breath.

"'And when He had opened the seventh seal, there was silence in heaven about the space of half an hour,'" said Poe, who loved the Book of Revelation, of Saint John of Patmos, more than any other sacred text.

Two men in rubber aprons took down the body, as Nicodemus and Joseph of Arimathea had done the murdered Christ from his gibbet. They laid him—tenderly, I thought—on a barrow and wheeled him inside the prison to wash his corpse. It would end in potter's field or, perhaps, in

Mütter's own museum after the bones had been rid of their flesh and blood. I wondered what Vogel and he would find to talk about during the long hours of darkness when the door to the exhibits was shut. Edgar would know. He'd make a story out of it, damn him: a comic piece of minstrelsy, with Vogel playing the part of Bones, Holtz, or Heinz, that of Tambo, with Poe as Mr. Interlocutor—pedantic middle-man to their befuddled and black-faced end men.

> INTERLOCUTOR: Brother Bones.
>
> BONES: Yessuh, Mr. Interlocutor?
>
> INTERLOCUTOR: You seem down in the mouth this morning. Didn't you sleep well?
>
> BONES: No, suh. The new man was gnashin' his teeth all night.
>
> INTERLOCUTOR: Did you have a night-mare, Brother Tambo?
>
> TAMBO: Yessuh. I dreamt I was once a man and had come to grief and dust.
>
> INTERLOCUTOR: As do we all—correct, Brother Bones?
>
> BONES: Ain't that the truth!
>
> TAMBO (anguished): I can't feel my face!
>
> INTERLOCUTOR: There's nothing anymore to feel.
>
> TAMBO: I wisht I had a mirror to see myself in!
>
> INTERLOCUTOR: There's nothing more to see, Tambo. Isn't that right, Bones?

BONES *(to Tambo)*: Not in Mr. Mütter's
charnel house, there ain't.

TAMBO *(wistfully)*: I can almost remember
the world. . . . *(Bones laughs.)* What's
to be done, suhs?

BONES: Nothin' to be done. We is all past
doin'.

TAMBO *(whispering)*: I sees a bloody knife
and the hangman's rope.

BONES: Don't distress yourself, Brother
Tambo. They's just figments of the
Interlocutor's mind. He's a writer
man. He makes things up in his head.

TAMBO: Am I only a thought in his mind,
then?

BONES: We boff is. *(Shakes his head sadly.)*
No happy endings here. *(Tambo
weeps.)* He's cryin' again, Mr. Interlocutor, even though he ain't got no
eyes or tears.

INTERLOCUTOR *(brightly)*: Cheer up,
Brother Tambo! Mr. Bones.

BONES: Yessuh?

INTERLOCUTOR: Let's sing Tambo one of
our humorous songs.

BONES: Tha's a good idea, Mr.
Interlocutor!

BONES and MR. INTERLOCUTOR *(singing
together)*:

> Love, sweet love, is the poet's
>   theme—
> Love, sweet love, is the poet's dream;
> But all of this of which they sing
> Is only a nightmare, a dreadful dream.

(Tambo weeps all the more.)

BONES: He didn't like that song much,
    Mr. Interlocutor, suh.
INTERLOCUTOR: Then I'll sing him
    another one.

*(Singing, while Bones accompanies him with
    the bone "clackers.")*

> Now the tambo and the bones are
>   forever laid away,
> The fiddle and the banjo are unstrung;
> But I often heave a sigh for the happy
>   days gone by,
> And the times I used to have when I
>   was young.

(Tambo weeps some more.)

The wind had emptied its cheeks with a sigh that blew flakes of snow against my own. It had begun to snow again. Turning from the iron door opening onto the street to take a last look at the place where we had stood—a threshold between life and its dismal opposite—I saw how the sunken footsteps in the yard and on the gallows' stairs had nearly filled with snow. In a moment, it would be as if none of us had ever walked there and trembled in fear and impatience. The door shut behind us. Life was suddenly everywhere in the street, boisterous and gay. Edgar took my arm. I shook it off and hurried down the pavement.

"You look terrible, Edward," said Dr. Mütter while I was hanging up my coat and hat on the clothes tree in a corner of the dissecting room.

I noticed that the aspidistra on the windowsill was dead. This is a dreadful place to spend one's days, I said to myself. I should have let my brother find me a job on the wharf. I'd rather dream of dank holds and bilges than atrocities. I could as well have been a grave digger or an undertaker's boy as the keeper of a chamber of horrors.

"I went to a hanging," I said, unable to hold his gaze, which always put me in mind of a straight pin through an insect's thorax.

"With Edgar Poe?"

I nodded.

"I'm told he has acquaintances throughout the Philadelphia netherworld," said Mütter. "He's a regular visitor to the city morgue and God knows what other unsavory haunts. I suppose he must do so for the sake of his art. Had he been Dana, Cooper, or Melville, his disposition would be no less grim, but, relieved of his penchant for the sordid, his literary efforts would be more wholesome. Still, you have to admire him. I do, for we have something in common."

I didn't bother to ask him what. Honestly, Moran, I was sick to death of Edgar Poe and his "literary efforts."

"Did you learn anything useful?" asked Mütter.

"Learn anything?" I repeated stupidly.

"At this morning's hanging. I understood you to have an interest in anatomy. I can think of no better introduction to the subject—short of dissecting a corpse—than a hanging."

Mütter liked to make unconventional remarks. Usually, I would laugh to show him my loyalty—a different thing altogether from servility, at least in my own mind as it was constituted then. That afternoon, however, I made my face a mask suitable to the numbness of my heart. The spectacle had shaken me, Moran! I had yet to be hardened—coarsened—by war's butchery and the bloody "pit" of the operating theater. I wanted a drink and might have thrown a beaker's worth of medicinal alcohol down my gullet to anesthetize my frayed nerves. There were times when I felt myself to be the boy I was and wanted others to see me thus. Feeling my eyes begin to moisten in self-pity, I grew angry. We act by contrariety, Moran. We advance and retreat.

Mütter pretended not to notice my distress. "It's fascinating to see the human body at the limits of its structural integrity. In his own way, the hangman is an anatomical empiricist. If he makes the rope too long, the condemned man's head will be torn from his shoulders at the end of the drop; too short, and his neck won't break. Death won't be instantaneous—that is, merciful—but an agony of slow asphyxiation."

I left him to his drollery and walked into the exhibits room. I had a mind to take Vogel from the shelf and search his eye sockets for news of his brother Heinz, or Holtz. But I shook off the fancy. At that moment, I wanted nothing to do with Poe or Mütter or anyone else whose mind was not commonplace and whose wit would make a woman blanch. The doctor followed after me.

"You must learn to ignore it," he said. I gave him my blankest look. "The disgust, the dismay a good soul feels in the presence of obscene horrors, which are everywhere. You've only to open your eyes, Edward, and see—around every corner, underneath every stone, just beyond the vanishing point—what cannot be endured. But we must endure it, Edward—you must if you intend to become a physician. I know that's your ambition, and it is a noble one. I can help you. But you won't last—I would not have lasted for as long as I have—without a counterbalancing emotion: humor, irreverence, blasphemy, even. Do you see what I mean?"

I did, but I kept silent.

His disappointment was evident. Squirming, I felt the specimen pin of his penetrating gaze.

"You'll learn stoicism, Edward, or you will surely fail. If you had Edgar Poe's gift, you might write your horrors down and make a few dollars. I don't foresee a long or happy life for our friend. By the way, I invited Edgar to view the restorative surgery on Nathaniel Dickey's face. He's written that he'll come. I knew he would. The organ where his curiosity is seated is degenerate. As a surgeon, I would advise him to have it out, if only I knew where to cut. He'd refuse, of course. Men like him must cling to their perversities; they are what define them. Can you imagine Poe as a clergyman? No, not even a Unitarian. Demons have eaten into his vitals; his heart is cankered. His reason, I suspect, is perpetually in the balance. I wouldn't recommend his life or his example. You're better off here, where hearts no longer beat or minds think."

He handed me a slip of paper. "I've an errand for you. Take the dogcart to the Union Street pier. I ordered some birds that will keep you busy: three conjugal pairs of domesticated rock pigeons from Belgium."

I stuffed a bill of sale into my pocket and put on my coat and hat again. I would rather have confessed to murder than to show Mütter my curiosity, which, at that moment, I regarded as something sordid and repugnant—a voyeurism broader than a man's natural interest in sex—an unnatural, shameful fascination for what is properly left to obscurity. I was a Christian, Moran. I suppose I still am in whatever organ belief, however adulterated, resides. I don't think we can ever be rid of doctrines instilled in us in childhood. Our characters are tells: history's deposits laid down one on top of another by time. Outwardly, we are modern men and women, but you have only to dig to discover the primitive state from which we came. While I mock hell, in my marrow, I quake in fear of it.

The cobbled streets jarred me as I drove the cart, on iron wheels, eastward toward the river. I let the horse have its way, being in no hurry to get back to the college. Flaming in the western-facing windows of the city's buildings, the sun felt almost mild on my face. The wind having lessened, the afternoon was warm for January. The snowy lots on either side of the road were ugly with ashes and soot, the curbstones stained yellow by horses' stale.

I gave myself up to passing fancies of a kind alien to Poe's and Mütter's grotesque imaginations: fresh snow in the shape of an elephant's head clinging to the brick wall of the *American Sentinel* building on Sansom Street; my father's dark, mysterious member exposed when he climbed out of the galvanized tub in the shed, soapy rivulets streaming from his hairy body; my mother's face when she leaned toward the candlelight to turn the page of her book; the tattooed anchor livid on my brother's arm; Ida's pretty neck, white and slender as a swan's where it rose demurely above the collar of her Sunday dress. I realized with a start that I wanted very much to see her. Did I care for her, or was she only an antidote for my poisoned heart? I would always be unsure of myself in love, that most complicated of emotions.

I tied the horse to a hitching post outside the warehouse and stood awhile on the wharf to watch the river traffic. The Delaware was already darkening as the sun declined toward evening. I imagined that the Atlantic, on the far side of New Jersey, was already drained of light, its wide beach gray as ash. I watched stevedores walk carefully down a ship's wet gangway, their backs bent under burlap sacks of coffee beans. I sensed weakness in my body's small bones and felt inferior to those brawny men and afraid that I'd prove unequal to the toils of life. I wished that, like my brother, Franklin, I'd inherited my father's sturdy frame and regretted that I'd treated Dr. Mütter coldly earlier in the afternoon. At all costs, I must hold on to my position at the medical college, for I might not find another so comfortable. The horse nickered and pawed at the snow, which had grown on the post tops, the railings, and on the docked ships' sheets and rigging like a delicate white moss. Out in the channel, a clipper, riding high in the water, sped upriver toward the mills; three sailors hauled on a line to warp a packet boat against the current; and steaming out from the Camden dock, a ferry commenced its crossing.

Inside the shipping company's warehouse, which smelled pleasantly of oakum, tar, hemp, Indian spices, and coffee, a clerk, his fingers and cuffs inky, was writing in a ledger, all the while cursing the clotted nib. I slid the bill of sale across the counter, and, after leisurely finishing an entry, he deigned to raise his eyes to mine.

"First time I ever saw pigeons come by boat from overseas." He spoke with the sarcasm of a man whom chance, fate, nepotism, or the civil service had made emperor of the tiniest of realms, who never missed an opportunity to lord it over anyone who happened there. I felt like cudgeling him with the marlin spike he used as a paperweight but tempered my resentment with the thought of those muscled stevedores who might come rushing to his aid. I nearly blushed to think how I must have looked to them in my dandy's rig and congress boots. "Ain't Philadelphia pigeons good enough, you had to send to Belgium for some?"

"They're for the chief surgeon of Jefferson Medical College," I said haughtily.

Unimpressed, the clerk grunted, rang a bell on the counter, and, when a colored man appeared from a back room, directed him to carry two wicker hampers out to the dogcart. I turned on my heel without another word to the sneering fellow and left him to his smudges.

I gave the negro a penny and climbed up onto the

seat. Inside the hampers, Mütter's pigeons mumbled and beat their stiff wings nervously against the wickerwork. I snapped the reins, and the horse clopped onto Front Street, its nostrils flaring at a sudden rankness of dead fish. At the end of a pier, a rope, made taut by the outbound current, had tightened around the neck of a rusty bollard capped with snow.

At the delivery door behind the college building, two porters carried the hampers inside, the jostled pigeons complaining. After having assured myself that they had survived the jolting trip from the wharf, I went to find Dr. Mütter, determined to make myself agreeable.

"I brought you your birds," I said affably.

"Excellent!" he replied, rubbing his hands together like an excited boy contemplating the destruction of a rat's nest. "I trust they're alive and well after their journey?"

"Yes, sir," I said, smiling plausibly.

"I had a coop built on the roof for them. You may have noticed it."

"No, sir, I didn't," I said, still smiling with an exaggerated cheerfulness. My jawbones were beginning to ache, as they will when you've been playing the Jew's harp.

"The birds will live and mate there."

"I'm curious, Dr. Mütter, what you mean to do with them."

"I want to know how it is they can find their way home."

"Can they, sir?"

"They're no ordinary pigeons, Edward. They've been bred to fly home from as far away as a thousand miles, even over mountains."

So that he would know that I was duly impressed, I whistled in astonishment.

"Science affirms a medium of attraction—ether, *spiritus*, pneuma, call it what you like—that conveys, across space, the influence of one thing on another. Newton described it as 'a subtle spirit which pervades and lies hid in all gross bodies; by the force and action of which spirit, particles of bodies attract one another.' It would explain the effect of the moon on tides and on the womb, the transmission of light, heat, and sound, the curious affinity of twins, the uncanny ability of some rare individuals to will objects to move as if by themselves, the eerie instances when a thought seems to jump wordlessly from one mind to another, the apparently collective intelligence of a flock of birds or a cloud of gnats that causes it to swerve en masse, perhaps the influence of facial features on character, and even the periodic incidence of various diseases."

My eyes about to wander to the window, I fixed them purposefully on Mütter's own.

"Mesmer wrote of the effect of celestial gravitation on physiology. While a student in Paris, I attended Deleuze's lectures and was persuaded of the existence of a magnetic fluid—Mesmer's 'imponderable fluid' distributed uniformly throughout the universe, which makes actions at a distance possible. If there's a soul, Edward, perhaps it resides in that magnetism, and evil—to speak in the idiom preferred by our friend Edgar Poe—in contagious effluvia."

He grew pensive and played absentmindedly with a jawbone, which he kept on his desk. The mandible, with its row of uneven teeth, had been dug up in a field by the college porter's dog. Nothing more of what had once been a woman in her twenties had been recovered, although the police had turned over the lot with rakes and shovels. If her skull had been found intact, she might have called to her scattered remains. In my mind's eye, I watched them tunnel through the earth and make her whole again. Such were the morbid thoughts of a young man—a fickle moon orbiting the poles of the worldly Thomas Mütter and otherworldly Edgar Poe.

"What does not bear thinking about, however, is that human beings are no better than marionettes. There must be a countervailing individual will—a mind able to resist."

Dr. Mütter hoped to find a faculty of navigation in his pigeons independent of animal magnetism or the body's "factors," units of inheritance proposed a decade earlier by Gregor Mendel. He wished to show men and women that they were more than automatons doing the bidding of stronger wills than theirs, or of a legacy willed them by the past, or of the stars. He wanted to prove that the birds *chose* to fly home. I've always thought that this same ambition was the true meaning of his plastic operations: to free us from the urgencies of plan or accident or, at least, to oblige us to grapple with them, however unequal we may be to the struggle and uncertain of the outcome.

How naïve! Poe, the pessimist and fatalist, would entertain the idea and quickly dismiss it, saying, "Each human being believes that he occupies the center of the *universe*, but it is only the center of a *spider's web*. He's blessed if he lives and dies in ignorance of his ensnarement."

I was too tired and, frankly, too bored to hear more

of Mütter's disquisition. He handed me several pages of handwritten instructions for the birds' care, feeding, breeding, and training and then bid me good night. I gave him mine and left him to his thoughts.

Outside, the lamps had been lit; their lights fell uncertainly on streets and sidewalks, any suggestion of warmth in their yellowish glimmer dampened by newly fallen snow. The college building hulked, black against a bleached sky, its windows dark except for those of Dr. Mütter's laboratory. Tomorrow, he would operate on Nathaniel Dickey's face.

I tightened the muffler around my neck and walked to the streetcar that would take me to a Bridesburg rooming house "for Christian ladies," near the Frankford Creek ferry dock, where Ida lodged in dreary austerity. I hurried like a man pursued, the hunter a nameless anxiousness harrying me through the ether.

Ida and I had been childhood sweethearts, living, at the time, a street apart in Northern Liberties. Her father and mine had been friends and workers, both of them, in the cotton mill. She'd been a pretty, lively girl; was pretty yet, but the liveliness had gone. Maybe it was the inevitable result of having grown into a woman—she seemed much older than I, though she was just twenty—or perhaps the religion of the Calvinists had sobered her. There was no gaiety in her, and she talked of God as though He were a resident of Mrs. DeVries's boardinghouse on Ann Street, a man—venerable and avuncular—who shared in their fish or mutton at the ladies' dinner table. It was, I knew, a mistake to visit her. There would be little comfort and even less joy as we sat together in the parlor, with its confused scent of pine needles, moth flakes, lavender sachet, and asafetida bags.

No, Moran, it wasn't desire that drew me to her that chilly night—the chaste particles of our two bodies attracted by a subtle spirit, to borrow from Sir Isaac Newton, who understood animal magnetism, if not love. I was afraid to be alone; to have gone home and sat with my mother or to have gone to Noonan's taproom to drink with Franklin would not have made me feel any less lonely or afraid.

What was I afraid of?

I had heard too much talk from Poe and Mütter about things better left unsaid. Life is complicated and dangerous without making it more so by intimations of mysterious, unseen forces that might not bode well. I'm a doctor. I talk to other doctors. I read medical journals. I've peered through a microscope and seen van Leeuwenhoek's bacteria and Karl Weigert's malevolent stains. How lovely, even beautiful, are those organisms that cause us to sicken and die! I shudder at the thought of them! I wish I'd never seen them. It's heresy or backwardness to regret knowledge. We eradicate sickness; we lengthen the span of life by making visible what once was invisible. But it doesn't help me fall asleep at night to imagine the teeming world of illness and death. To count bacilli like sheep going over a stile. At heart, I'm a simple doctor, who feels happy and useful setting broken bones, listening to a man's or a woman's chest, and examining the sputum. As ghastly as it sounds, there was something clean and satisfying about taking off a man's shattered arm or leg in a field hospital. The moment was clear, unambiguous, calm. I sawed the blasted bone and cauterized the wound and knew that I'd done a workmanlike job of saving the fellow's life. But that's enough of this, Moran.

I went to visit Ida, and we sat in the boardinghouse parlor, speaking of this and that—childhood reminiscences, her day in the knitting mill, my afternoon jaunt to the river, the cold, the snow, the Methodists' split over slavery. I said nothing about the morning's hanging. It was one of the things I wanted to forget. The clock on the wall marked the tedium of my visit. I wanted to take her hand. That would have been enough. But my will had no power over my arm's muscles. Or maybe it was that my muscles would not answer the call of my will. For whatever reason, I left my hand where it was, on the arm of the chair, covered with a tatted antimacassar. The rag rug on the floor between us might as well have been the ocean or an Arctic chasm. I smiled at her, and she answered it with one of her own—sincere, well-meant, and virginal. I looked at the clock, the oil lamp, the miserly fire in the grate, the picture of John Calvin on the wall. I could think of nothing else to say, and so I wished her good night and, having put on my coat and hat, walked all the way to my mother's house—pondering the homing faculty of pigeons as I passed through the pneuma of an icy rain.

As soon as MÜTTER HAD FINISHED operating on Nathaniel Dickey, I left the theater and, without a word to Poe, hurried to the pigeon coop. I dreaded his enthusiasm, the fervent interest he would show in "Mütter's miracle." He'd insist on teasing from the tangle of his recent sensations a thread of sense to dwell on—glory in—and to deduce from it a narrative. Whether it was the somberness of the short winter days or the unwelcome impressions lately made on my immature mind, I felt a kind of bruise on the soft tissues of my sensibility that wanted nursing in solitude, or, at most, in the company of Mütter's pigeons, which possessed their own acute sensitivity but did not confide in me their inner peace or turmoil.

Later on, after I had succumbed to Poe's influence, we would spend long evenings by some tavern fire arguing the result of Mütter's surgery. Poe and I believed that—having been born an outcast and sentenced to a profound estrangement from his kind, a tormented being whose disfigured face relegated him to a shadow life—Nathaniel Dickey must have also been *inwardly* deformed, his mind turned from thoughts of ordinary life, his disposition soured, and his soul—let the word stand—in jeopardy. Our surmise was no more than physiognomy, which we accepted without question. In my opinion, however, Dr. Mütter had done more than to operate on a face: He'd rescued the man who had worn it like a mask covering his true self.

Poe, of the contrary opinion, could not allow himself to find a happy outcome in tragedy. To his mind, redemption was impossible in this life or the next. Humankind was damned at the outset—if not by original sin, as he didn't think in orthodox Christian terms—then by congenital perversity, wickedness at the heart of the race, a self-regard at the center of each one of us that makes us blind to others' selves and deaf to their pleas.

I argued against his cynicism, but his unsentimental

attitudes were too strong, his defense of them too vigorous
and articulate for me to counter. I was hardly yet a man
and could only stumble after him as he rushed impetu-
ously forward through a thicket of ideas and a wildness of
talk. I would soon give up. In all my dealings with Poe,
I suspect that he saw the world from the viewpoint of his
art, which was a universe in miniature, obedient to its
own logic and to its own physical laws. The gravitational
attraction between his fiction's characters and the places
where they led their lives was stronger than that of actuality. His tales bristle with their own charge.

"Edgar Poe was looking for you," said Mütter, startling
me by his abrupt appearance at the door to the coop. "I
had the feeling he wanted to talk to you about the operation. His eyes were fairly glittering with excitement, or else
wickedness."

I dug the scuttle into an opened burlap bag and filled the
trough with dried feed corn.

"He's not a man you can ignore or hide from," said Mütter, buttoning his coat against the cold. "He'll find you
whether you choose to meet with him or not."

I knew what he meant: Poe's thought would seek me out
and, by the affinity of our two minds, which was already
apparent, entangle me. It was a fantastic notion, of course,
and hardly in keeping with the sensible work I did at the
college of medicine. But it was true nonetheless.

"I'm troubled in his presence," I grumbled.

Mütter laughed. "It is always so in cases of adoration."

"I don't adore him!" I nearly shouted, incensed.

"What, then?" Mütter's eyes sought mine. Had I been a

pan of water, I'd have come to a boil with the intensity of
his gaze.

I spoke without hesitation, aware for the first time of the
quality of my attraction to the strange, magnetic personality named Edgar Allan Poe. "I fear him."

Mütter shrugged. "Fear and adoration are part and parcel
of the same thing." I must have given him a quizzical look,
because he continued in explanation. "The helpless feeling
we have for great men or women." I would have scoffed,
but he left me no time to object. "Edgar Poe is a great man
who has in him the tragic seeds of his downfall. I've said it
before, Edward: He will not last."

I shuddered—an involuntary movement I would often
make when I thought of Poe.

"How are the birds?" asked Mütter, whose genius con-
tained an element of caprice.

"They seem all right."

"Have they settled in?"

"Seems so."

I looked at the fresh boards caulked with tar, the chicken
wire, where wisps of down clung, the planked floor carpeted
with manure, and the nesting boxes waiting for offspring.
In May of the following year, I'd take the pigeons on the
first of their trips away from home and, that fall, consign
the wicker hampers to the Burlington and Bristol Railway
freight agent to load onto a wagon car. The birds would be
released at ever-more distant towns, whence they'd fly back
to their roost. However Mütter would cover their eyes with
falconry hoods or their nostrils with paraffin to disable per-
ception, they still found their way to the coop again. Only

a few were ever lost to storms or exhaustion, to hawks or hunters mistaking them for passenger pigeons, which are delicious roasted.

No . . . it wasn't *those* birds; they ended badly. Other pigeons would take their place, multiply, and row home through the ether. All during 1845, Mütter tried to discover how they navigated, unerringly, back to the college roof, as if by nostalgia for their mates, their young, the smell of pine boards and creosote, the stink of their own dung, the pattern of grit and dried corn scattered on the floor, for the familiar images mirrored by their tiny brains, for their phantom selves milling peevishly inside the coop while their real selves circled the sky, waiting to feel their way home. *Home,* Moran. I doubt you feel about home even so much as a pigeon does—not for the Brooklyn tenement where you scrabbled for light and air and affection till you were old enough to escape. Nostalgia is a sickness whose cause is time and whose remedy is death; your unhappy childhood is proof against it.

Mütter studied the brains of numerous pigeons after I had wrung their necks—the most humane method of dispatching them—but he could find nothing to account for their navigational ability. To call it "instinctual" would have been as unsatisfactory as "ethereal." I suppose that he'd hoped to discover an organ of free will. Poe—incurable fantasist!—called him "the Martin Luther of medicine," in that he wanted to remove God from His heaven and put Him in one of the heart's small rooms. Mütter published his disappointing conclusions in *The Zoist: A Journal of Cerebral Physiology and Mesmerism.*

"It must be as Newton thought," he wrote. "Affinity acts at a distance on unseen particles inherent in objects by a transmission of influence analogous to rings spreading across the surface of a pond. Homing pigeons must 'sense,' in the imponderable fluid within the hollows of their bones, the magnetic attraction of home *and be irresistibly drawn to it*."

Edgar had reached the same conclusion without needing to slaughter birds. He relished the fantastic obverse of the doctor's conjecture: The pigeon coop's magnetic particles answered to the birds' own. Had it not been ponderous and anchored to the roof, it might have moved, albeit slowly, like an inchworm through a field, toward them. I know Poe to have been at work on a revenger's tale in which a corpse, left in a shallow grave, did, after many years, make its way finally to the murderer of its flesh and blood self and strangle him with its bony fingers.

Dr. Mütter concluded his article with an admission: "While I cannot accept Mesmer's magnetic cures, his 'artificial tides,' or the mysterious grant of hypnotic power given to 'operatives,' I acknowledge the existence of a transmitting energy, a gravitational attraction among all animate and inanimate objects. One might almost say that each thing in the universe possesses a will that exerts its influence on every other thing, successfully or not according to its strength."

By his book and by his pigeons, Mütter had hoped to refute the mesmerists and win for our kind a freedom from outside interference, from predestination and its hell, but he had failed. There would be healing but no magic reformation or personal redemption in the pit. In universal terms, we would continue to be in the hands of circumstances beyond human control. Beaten, he renounced metaphysics and devoted himself once more to medical science and its monsters.

TWO OR THREE DAYS LATER, I received a note from Edgar Poe, sent in care of Dr. Mütter, asking me to visit him at home at six o'clock that night. I could think of no good reason to decline, except my own unease, and, at the end of the workday, I took a car to the city's Spring Garden district. The weary horses hauled us through the whirling streets, flakes of new snow like St. Elmo's fire luminous in the lamplight, snow drifting on windward pavements, the windows of commercial establishments dead in their sashes, except for an occasional flicker of candles where a lawyer, an accountant, or a merchant still sat at his desk. The meal we shared was a meager one. Edgar had not been paid for his story "The Black Cat," published in August. Mrs. Clemm had yet to receive her widow's pension for the month. The house was dark and cold. The parrot's cage was covered against the drafts; the silent bird dreaming, perhaps, of Cuba or Africa. I wished I had not come. By now, my brother would have had the hearth fire blazing for the sake of my mother, who suffered from rheumatism.

After dinner, Edgar and I smoked long clay pipes like Dutchmen, while Virginia and Mrs. Clemm kept to the kitchen, near the woodstove. I told him of my car ride through the snowy night, and he was reminded of what

Francis Bacon had written: "There is no excellent beauty that hath not some strangeness in the proportion." He talked about his favorite subjects: hate, which he said was a purer emotion than love, having only a single cause; murder, which was what passed for intimacy in those who could not love; and damnation, in his opinion, the only apt theme for an American writer. He liked, he said, to write about people at the end of their rope, stretched to the breaking point, who must necessarily die or else go mad with the strain. As if to illustrate his point, he ground his teeth on his pipe's clay stem, making a noise like chalk screeching against a slate.

"Life is best seen in extremis," he said, knocking the bowl of his pipe on the cast-iron fender to rid it of ash; "just as a tree is more easily measured when it's down."

I told him, in my turn, about Dr. Mütter's pigeons and about Mesmer and Deleuze. Poe already knew, of course, about pneuma and *spiritus* and acknowledged their importance.

"How else, except by a universal and diffuse atmosphere, can one divine the nature of other people, receive intimations of an unseen world, sense the presence of the dead, dowse for water, or feel another's pain and sorrow? The genuine medium or spiritualist—God knows, Edward, there are abundant fakers and frauds—is simply a person whose mesmerist faculty is more highly developed than it is in ordinary men and women. I sometimes think it is so in me. It's difficult to explain otherwise how I write—the almost trancelike state that comes over me in the heat of composition. My hand moves at the behest of some other's intelligence—I can't say whose. At such times, I'm no more than an amanuensis taking dictation." He went to the desk and opened a newspaper. "A mesmerist is in town this week at the Athenaeum on Sixth Street, near St. James Place. Karl Menz, one of Elliotson's disciples. I'm thinking of reporting on the demonstration for *The American Whig Review*. You ought to go, as well, Edward. Perhaps Dr. Mütter will pay for your admission. My means, as you know, are slender."

Poe grew thoughtful, and, in a silence punctuated by the detonations of a log alive with sap, the fitful scratching of a tree branch against the front room's window, and, from the kitchen, the low voices of the women, which sounded, at a distance, like whispering, I fell into a stupor. Poe took up his pen and began to write on a piece of foolscap. The room was warm, and I closed my eyes, listening to his pen, like a crochet hook, turn the strands of his thought into something new.

Mütter not only paid for my ticket to Menz's "Magnetic Salon" but he also accompanied Poe and me there. In return, I provided both men with evidence, if not of the mesmerist's power to entrance, then of my own susceptibility to another's will. Two hundred people or so turned out for the spectacle. How many were serious in their interest, how many had come to gawk at subjects pitting their wills against the mesmerist's, as though the séance were a wrestling match or a cockfight, I couldn't have said. Edgar and Mütter were in earnest, of course, although their interests in the contest of minds fought in the garish limelight of the Athenaeum's stage were different: Mütter sought a truth about the human mind; Poe, about his fictional characters. I didn't know then that the doctor's truth and that of the artist might be different, perhaps even opposed.

Menz began his performance with a learned introduction to Franz Anton Mesmer and his science, which was, I felt, merely a justification for the spectacle—the magic show—itself. The spectators could flatter themselves that they were improving their minds, and I noticed only an occasional restlessness betraying their impatience. The evening was like an illustrated book on the Fiji Islanders, purporting to be a scholarly work of ethnology, while its real intent was to purvey to gentlemen the sight of the naked breasts of island girls. There were a number of "acts," differing hardly at all from those of a variety or vaudeville show. I performed in two.

The first, which caused my two friends much amusement, was a comic production of the miracle play of Noah and his ark, in which I took the part of an ass desperate to find its mate in the aftermath of the Flood. During a late supper after Menz's demonstration, they told me that I had brayed forlornly and most convincingly.

"Your metamorphosis was not the result of the hypnotist's animal magnetism," said Mütter, his patrician nose inside a brandy snifter, "but the strength of your imagination. He merely led you by suggestion to your excellent impersonation."

He still had hopes of exalting the human will, of giving it preeminence over external forces—call them fate, accident, gratuitous election, or astrological tyranny.

"It made me think of Bottom's dream," said Poe, ever the man of letters.

Mütter smiled appreciatively.

My face and neck grew warm in embarrassment. I felt a pricking on my cheek. I hadn't read *A Midsummer Night's Dream*, but I knew I was an object of ridicule. I concentrated on my plate of oysters, as if I'd never seen their like before.

"Mockery aside, I paid you a compliment, Edward," said Mütter in a voice that never failed to appease the envy of his colleagues or comfort the uncertainty of his patients. I'd heard him use that same honeyed tone in the pit when, beside himself with his terror of the surgeons' instruments, a patient had shivered uncontrollably and wept.

"How's that?" asked Edgar.

"An unimaginative man would not have been receptive to Menz's hypnotic suggestions . . . his willpower. You cannot hypnotize a stone. I'll leave it to you, Edgar, to decide which is stronger: will or imagination."

"Imagination, of course!"

"I'd have wagered on your answer," said Mütter.

Fiddling with my fork, I pretended not to follow the conversation.

"Art is one of the few things in this world that will not bend to the will—one's own or another's," said Edgar. "Only the imagination, our most sovereign faculty, can move the hand to paint, to write, to compose. The muse is deaf to all else. In my case, my fancy is rich, my wallet poor."

He pulled on his coat sleeves to hide his worn cuffs.

"Bravo!" cheered Mütter, lifting his glass in recognition

of Poe's artistry, which, as he'd told me more than once, he admired. "Tonight is my treat," he said, self-satisfied as a man with the wherewithal to be generous in company. "And you, Edward, how would you have answered the question?"

"The imagination, as far as I can see," I said, glancing at Poe, "does a man little good—or his poor wife, either."

I was thinking of Virginia, sitting by the kitchen stove, with a wool shawl around her frail shoulders.

Poe gave me a secret look, partly shame, partly resentment. Mütter grinned devilishly. Incapable of meeting Edgar's chilly stare, I studied the palm of my hand, as if I expected to see my future written there.

A suave diplomat, Mütter changed the subject. "The business with the mirror I found even more intriguing."

At Menz's command, I had succeeded in making an ass of myself a second time that night.

Yes, I was still in a trance. I had fallen into a deep sleep at the start of the comedy. Dr. Mütter's compliment aside, I'd been an easy prey to the mesmerist's harrying gaze, the pendulum of his gold watch and chain, his thought as it traveled through the magnetic fluid and rooted in the organ of my imagination.

I laid my fork noisily on the pewter plate, by now heaped with empty oyster shells. "What mirror?" I was very much annoyed.

"You don't remember?" asked Poe.

"Of course he doesn't," said Mütter.

I didn't recall anything of my performance on the Athenaeum's stage. I had awakened at Menz's command, my mind a blank, as is usual for a mesmerist's subject. I know what happened to me only because Poe and Mütter told me afterward.

"Ordered to fall in love with the next person you saw, you fell in love with yourself—your image reflected in the cheval glass that had been hidden behind a velvet drape."

"You were 'enamored of an ass'!" cried Poe, pleased with himself.

He was, I noted with satisfaction, barely sober. I hoped he would disgrace himself, and promised myself I'd have nothing further to do with him. I was angry at them both, but of the two men, Mütter offered the better chance for advancement. I was an opportunist then, as all ambitious young men are.

"You could almost say that the person in the mirror mesmerized you, Edward," said Mütter, becoming serious.

"Doppelgänger," said Poe, guzzling another neat whiskey.

I watched in fascination the motions of his throat and pictured it encircled by a noose or sliced with a razor.

"Indeed," said Mütter.

And then Poe recited a paragraph from his story "William Wilson" that ended "'From his inscrutable tyranny did I at length flee, panic-stricken, as from a pestilence; and to the very ends of the earth *I fled in vain*.' Doppelgänger; there's no getting away from it."

From the tavern's four corners, patrons craned their necks to discover the source of the disturbance. Embarrassed, Mütter bid Poe hush; the doctor was one of the city's illustrious, who, by his dress and deportment, had pledged himself to respectability despite a keen interest in medical rarities and freaks.

"I don't believe in your 'miracle,' *Dr.* Mütter," said Poe with a spitefulness distilled of too many malt whiskeys. "For us, there's no wriggling off the hook—not once we bite. And we all do bite. The bait dangled before our eyes is too delectable to resist. Our wills are weak, our imaginations too alive."

"It's time to go," said Mütter. "Edgar, can I give you a ride home in my carriage? I've arranged for Edward to spend the night, what's left of it, at my house."

His urbanity amazed me, but I understood that he wanted to remove "the unpleasantness" from the genteel precincts, where his reputation preceded him, with as much alacrity and poise as he could manage. He wanted to bundle the drunkard into his buggy and fly.

"I'd be honored, *sir,*" replied Poe, pronouncing the final word with a southern drawl and bowing like a gentleman at a cotillion and not a besotted poet in a Philadelphia tavern.

At that, we scraped back our chairs and, having paid the bill and a little more besides to lessen the landlord's displeasure, went outside into the cold, sobering air.

Philadelphia, February 1844

"You and Edgar are more alike than you suppose," said Mütter while his wife, Mary, a shy, pious woman, quietly poured us tea.

Are the wives of great men always this demure? I asked myself. I wouldn't care to be married to a tyrant and a shrew. I was weak-willed—last night's farce at the Magnetic Salon had shown me how weak. A bad wife would devour me. Even then, I wanted a "peaceable kingdom" of my own, but I knew that a woman like Mary or Ida would soon weary me with her goodness. I didn't want to make a bad marriage, Moran, so I made none at all.

I looked at the sumptuous room: the cheerful, generous fire, the bright andirons and screen, the luster of polished Regency furniture, the elegant plates and accessories of the table—so very different from the Poes' mismatched and dilapidated furnishings. I wouldn't have been able then to judge such things, but nonetheless I had the impression, unformed by experience as it must have been, that this fine home on Delancey Street was a world apart from that other on North Seventh. I envied Dr. Mütter and wanted to be like him. I thought that one day I might. Hadn't he promised that I would enter medical school if I worked hard and continued to show an aptitude? Eagerness—that's what the doctor liked to see in his students. I was bent on showing him how eagerly I wanted the life of a medical man, not to mention the rewards it would bring me. On that sunny winter morning, I let my mind drift among the golden motes of wishful thinking.

Mütter wanted to talk about Edgar Poe. "He has all the afflictions of his type," he said, spreading mulberry preserves on a piece of toast. "Melancholia, obsessiveness, destructiveness, intense self-regard, an addictive nature, a weakness of will coupled with a powerful, outlandish imagination."

"And you think I am like *him*?" I asked, having to control a sudden resentment.

"In kind, but nothing at all like him in degree. You will suffer a little; he will suffer much. Mary, what do you say to a face like my young friend's here?"

She blushed and replied, "He has a pleasant face and a kind one, I think."

"And what would the tea leaves say of him?"

"That he will live long and happily."

"There!" said Mütter, with his most winning smile. "Mary's instincts are infallible. You have nothing to worry about, Edward." He drank his tea, set the cup on its saucer, and went on. "But, like it or not, you and our Mr. Poe have an affinity. What was it he recited to us? 'From his inscrutable tyranny did I at length flee, panic-stricken, as from a pestilence; and to the very ends of the earth *I fled in vain.*' You cannot escape him, Edward. He is your doppelgänger. Why, even your Christian names reveal your fraternity! Edward, Edgar."

He laughed, and I did, too, to be agreeable. I was not happy with the conversation and changed it.

"What will you have me do today, Dr. Mütter?"

"Please excuse me, both of you," said Mary, rising from the table. "I must see Cook. Will you be home for dinner, Thomas?"

"Yes."

"Anything special you'd like?" she asked her husband, tucking a stray wisp of hair inside her old-fashioned "Sally cap."

"A shank of beef would be very nice, and some boiled potatoes."

Mary nodded, smiled politely at me, and withdrew to the kitchen.

"She does not like to hear the hospital discussed, in case I should forget myself and mention some grisly business. She is delicate."

I nodded sympathetically.

"I'm expecting several specimens from the city morgue. There are the pigeons—and Dr. Meigs has agreed that you shall give him whatever assistance you can this afternoon in the pit. I'm grooming you, my boy."

"I'm very grateful to you, sir."

"Don't disappoint me. And consider Mr. Poe as having a role to play in your education if for no other reason than he will afford you the opportunity to study the pathological mind firsthand."

"I'll keep an open mind, sir."

"Good fellow!"

Morning crept into the room with the obsequiousness of a medical student approaching the chief of surgery. Conversation adjourned, I gave myself up to the luxury of silence. I would have been content to remain so; Mütter, however, had something on his mind.

"Not long ago, Poe came to me with the most astonishing request: He wanted me to allow Menz to mesmerize one of my patients, Ernest Valdemar, who, he had found out through one of his cronies, was dying of Bright's disease. It was, he said, to be in the nature of an experiment—one I could, conceivably, profit from. He intended nothing less than to discover, through the dead offices of poor Valdemar, 'The undiscovered country, from whose bourn/ No traveller returns.' There was something in Edgar's face—a shamelessness that made me shudder.

"'Would you go even *there* to satisfy your curiosity?' I asked him.

"Poe smiled and said, 'There is *nowhere* I wouldn't go to learn the truth of the matter.'

"I'm a doctor, Edward. I've done things to make the antivivisections howl and virtuous young ladies blush. I've done them—sometimes reluctantly—for the advancement of science and the medical arts. My curiosity is not an idle one. I acknowledge the inviolable mystery of death and the proprieties surrounding it. I've dissected corpses, but I would not put a telegraph key into a dying man's hands and await his dispatches from the Other Side."

I made no answer, having none.

"Strange, these fellows whose life seems all in the mind," said Mütter as we rode in a cab toward the medical college. "From what I've read about Edgar, he's done little during his thirty-five years on earth. Oh, he was in the army—at Fort Independence, in Boston Harbor, and, later, in Charleston, where he was—fabulous coincidence!—an 'artificer,' meaning an enlisted man who assembles artillery shells. He would become an artificer of quite a different sort. Did you know he'd enlisted under an assumed name? Edgar A. Perry. I've known Poe only a short while, but I sense an instability in his character, a crisis of identity. It is often the case for orphaned children accepted into another's household. Good God! Edgar's birth parents were actors! What chance did he have to be his own person? You noticed last night how, when Menz asked the audience for volunteers, Poe did not offer his services. You'd have thought that a writer of the fantastic would have jumped at the chance to experience the trance state . . . to have let his mind sleep in order to know what dreams would follow. I watched him closely and saw on his face a contest between curiosity and fear."

"Fear of what?" I asked as the cab clattered into the college courtyard.

We walked across the wet stones and went inside the building.

"Of losing himself. You seemed to have no such fear last night when you kissed yourself in the mirror."

"I'm ashamed."

"You needn't be. You are irresistible."

Mütter laughed, and for a moment, I hated him.

Inside the laboratory, he put the kettle on for tea. The room was not yet warm, and we kept our coats buttoned up. It was the first of February; winter stretched before me, a gray and limitless prospect. Nourishing myself on a warming draft of self-pity, I imagined myself as one of Franklin's men, cold and miserable on the polar ice. I drizzled a little water on the plants, though they were past reviving.

"Poe lives his life in his own pages," said Mütter, opening the wooden chest of the Earl Grey he favored above all other teas. "Maybe that's sufficiently lively. I'd give a good deal of what I own to know where his words come from."

I didn't much care, but I pretended otherwise. Dividing

his attention between the teapot and his train of thought, Mütter continued.

"We say 'from his muse' or, just as enigmatically, 'from out of thin air' because we haven't a clue. If they are carried to him—a gift—by the *spiritus* or pneuma—call it what you like—in whose mind do they originate? A god's? A devil's? The Demiurge's? They have to come from someone or somewhere, Edward. We're bounded by a nutshell, and the imagination can only grope toward its congenital limitations. I fear we shall never know the origin of words, ideas, the ideal forms, any more than we'll fathom the mystery of the homing pigeon, regardless of how many tiny brains I will slice."

I was glad that my imagination was pedestrian. I wanted nothing to do with muses, no matter how pretty and seductive, with ghostly dictation, or with any other enigmas of a writer's secret and unhappy life.

"What is a doppelgänger?" I asked him, remembering the word Poe had used to ridicule me. The thought of my public humiliation on the stage of the Athenaeum the night before still rankled.

"An alter ego, a double, an evil twin, as in Edgar's story 'William Wilson.' To see oneself mirrored by another can be unnerving. But I shouldn't worry, Edward! Such unnatural phenomena belong to the world of gothic fiction—and, of course, in 'Mütter's museum.'" He laughed good-naturedly. "I know what the students say of me."

"Then you don't believe it's possible?" I found myself needing his assurance.

Say what he liked, I had seen my double and embraced it.

It was nothing more than a parlor trick, like one of Benjamin Franklin's "electricity parties" when the hair of his delighted guests would be made to rise by the cranking of an electrostatic generator or the discharge from a Leyden jar. But I had been in a trance, and mightn't I—by conjuration or suggestion—have been . . . I don't quite know how to put it, Moran, without sounding foolish or hysterical. In the lurid limelight, could I have become two persons, if only for an instant? Could my personality, which was thought to be inalienable and indissoluble, have split in two like Nathaniel Dickey's face before his surgery? On the Athenaeum stage, could I have given something of myself away?

"Do I believe that, somewhere in the world, one's double might exist?" said Mütter. "I would not say no, not absolutely. Chances are, in rare instances, doppelgängers do exist. Probability favors them. But the idea that one of the pair is an ill omen or a malignancy is utter nonsense. This is the year 1844, in an age of scientific progress! We have the telegraph, railroads, and daguerreotypes. I hope to see the day when a general anesthetic more reliable than ether or nitrous oxide will make our work painless."

We drank our cups of tea, and then Mütter left me to get on with the cataloguing of a fine specimen of pauper's brain. At noon, I went onto the roof to feed and water the birds. While there, Edgar Poe appeared like an apparition. Remembering my promise to Dr. Mütter to keep him under observation, as I would any interesting type, I dissembled my irritation.

"The good doctor said I might come up and see for myself your 'kingdom,'" he said.

I wasn't sure if he meant to mock me once again, but I smiled and introduced him to my subjects: two red-check hens, a pretty white, a gray, a blue, and a calico cock.

He listened to their peevish grumbling as they pecked at feed in an almost indifferent manner, like housewives unwilling to betray their admiration for a grocer's wares. Already, I'd grown to like "my" birds. You'd never guess that they had character—personalities, even—to see them, at the edges of your attention, waddling in the street or roosting under a railway bridge. Poe must have seen it immediately.

"They remind me of soldiers on furlough," he said, recalling a private memory of army life, perchance. "Dr. Mütter says he hopes to find out how they navigate."

"That's right," I said, carelessly picking molt from my trouser leg.

"By tiny compass. You must look for a miniature pocket, Edward." He went to stand by the window, where the homing birds might enter, and looked down into the street. The college building was four stories in height, and the view of the city took one's breath away. "Standing here, I'm reminded of Christ's temptation in the wilderness. 'Again, the devil taketh him up into an exceeding high mountain, and sheweth him all the kingdoms of the world, and the glory of them; And saith unto him, "All these things will I give thee, if thou wilt fall down and worship me."' How would you have answered the devil, Edward?"

"I'd tell him to go to hell."

"A straightforward answer," said Poe, and then he added thoughtfully, "I wonder if I would've answered likewise?"

"Aren't you a Christian?" I asked, made to feel uneasy once more by his unorthodoxy. I was never what you'd call a good Christian, Moran—not of the churchgoing and hymn-singing variety. Not like Ida or my mother or even my brother, Franklin, who would go to church on Sunday morning after a glorious carousal the night before.

"I believe in God and all the principalities and powers of light and darkness," said Poe. "I believe in Milton's *Paradise Lost.* Whether or not it can be regained is another story."

Always, he came back to literature, Moran, as surely as a homing pigeon does its coop.

"If Satan were to offer me knowledge . . . if he would show me the secrets of the human heart . . . tell me why we are as we are and behave as we do . . . Nathaniel Hawthorne has sent me a new tale, which is apposite to what we've been talking about."

With the theatricality of an actor, he recited a passage from memory. His back to me, he seemed to be speaking to passersby in the street, who, had they bothered to look up, would have thought him a madman or a prophet announcing ruin.

"'. . . before Ethan Brand departed on his search, he had been accustomed to evoke a fiend from the hot furnace of the lime-kiln, night after night, in order to confer with him about the Unpardonable Sin; the man and the fiend each laboring to frame the image of some mode of guilt, which could neither be atoned for, nor forgiven. And, with the first gleam of light upon the mountain-top, the fiend crept in at the iron door, there to abide in the intensest element of fire, until again summoned forth to share in the dreadful task of extending man's possible guilt beyond the scope of Heaven's else infinite mercy.'"

Edgar stood there gazing at the street, while I pretended to fuss over the birds and the appliances of their small domicile. Again, I felt a fascination for him growing in me like a cyst that would prove to be either benign or malignant. Dr. Mütter was right—he was nearly always so: There was an affinity between us, and I could not flee Poe, his influence, no matter how far I might run. And here we two were now, standing three feet apart, framed by the wide world and all its strangeness, with the little world of the pigeon coop at our feet, equally strange and marvelous. I knew in my heart I'd be obedient to his will and whims. He was my fiend and I his Ethan Brand. Even at this moment, Moran, I feel Poe's eyes on me, though he's been in his grave for more than a quarter of a century.

"Come with me tonight, Edward," he said casually, but I felt an injunction in his words.

I nodded, not caring to ask where. Unannounced destinations were part of the allure of my winter with Edgar Poe.

"I'll stop for you here, at the college's front gate, at half past six. We'll have a bite of supper and then be on our way."

I asked no questions.

"We'll be attending a small gathering of friends," he said, his back again turned to me. "Some very interesting fellows."

He left me to the solitude of my charges. They paid me no heed, existing for themselves alone, in their own universe of appetite, desire, and—who knows?—thought. They have brains—I've seen and weighed them. How else can they navigate with the skill of a mariner armed with a sextant? Even if they ride the mesmeric currents, they must—in my opinion—think.

That afternoon, I joined Dr. Meigs and his assistants in the surgical theater. To say that I was one of them would be untrue. I was only at the beginning of the road that would lead me to this Camden practice, tending Whitman's pleurisy. The stations of my particular cross have been painful enough: A man can't amputate in the field and not suffer more than a little, regardless of how he might try to distance himself by taking refuge in aesthetics. Strange word! But it's true, Moran. We doctors see beauty in a clean incision, a neat suture, even in the cauterized stump of flesh that will heal.

Dr. Meigs performed a trephination that afternoon. A hod of Belgian bricks at a building site had fallen on a mason's head. Meigs opened the skull and scraped out the bone splinters. While he worked, he told us of a reproduction he'd once seen of Hieronymus Bosch's painting *The Extraction of the Stone of Madness.* A medieval doctor, wearing a funnel hat, digs out a stone from a patient's cranium to cure him of his folly.

> *Meester snyt die keye ras*
> *Myne name is Lubbert Das.*
>
> Master, cut away the stone
> my name is Lubbert Das.

When we snickered at the primitivism of sixteenth-century medicine, Meigs chided us. "Gentleman, don't deceive yourselves." He made no further remark.

Lately, remembering his rebuke, I think how we were convinced, without room for doubt, of the truth of phrenology and physiognomy, sciences that are now questionable. Even the existence of an imponderable fluid is being debated. To me, its absence is unthinkable, Moran. We'd be like marionettes whose strings have been cut. Only a few extraordinary people are capable of self-government.

After the operation, which I observed, I cleaned the pit of blood and bandages, and then I wrote a report for Dr. Mütter.

"What have you learned?" he asked, having come to the end of it.

"That we can peer through a lens into a man's brain and see nothing of what makes him a man."

"Go on," he said flatly.

"Thoughts, instincts, inclinations, virtues, vices—none was visible through the opening in the patient's skull."

"And they never will be, Edward. It is our inscrutability that makes us a human being instead of a machine. We're physicians, not mechanics; our science is not Newton's. Maybe someday we'll be able to heal the mind, but the products of the mind must be left to philosophers and clergymen."

"Our thoughts can make us suffer," I said naïvely.

"We can do nothing about them." He was suddenly angry. "Do you want to be a man of science and medicine or a fantasist like your friend? The body is enough for us to worry about."

"Yes, Doctor."

"By the way, Mr. Fenzil, the instrument Dr. Meigs used

to raise the trephined bone was an elevator lever, not a scalpel." His manner had changed suddenly. "And is it asking too much for you to write legibly? It looks as if you'd written 'trepidation,' which might have been how you felt watching Dr. Meigs, but the surgery he performed was a trephination. Accuracy is essential. Muddle a prescription or a diagnosis and you can kill the patient."

"I'm very sorry, Dr. Mütter," I said, eying with a mixture of envy and contempt his gold filigreed buttons and purple velvet waistcoat.

"And well you should be."

He was right, of course, but I was in no mood to hear him. You know how it is, Moran: A young man would sooner scald himself than obey someone older and wiser who's warned him that, on no account, must he stick his hand in a pot of boiling water. There's no more vain and stubborn creature in God's creation than a boy who believes himself to be a man. You can die of such a delusion. Many have. I rewrote my notes, washed my hands and face, put on my coat and hat, doused the lights, and went outside to wait for Edgar Poe.

"You haven't asked me where we're going tonight," said Poe.

We were making a meal of bread, wurst, and bitter beer in a German saloon on Spring Garden Street. It was small, cramped, and rank with cigar smoke and rancid oil. Armed with knives and forks, stout men in worn suits of clothes sat talking loudly in Low German. The place was as different from the tavern where Mütter had taken us after Menz's shenanigans as a ballet is from a clog dance.

"Where are we going?" I asked, to have something to say. My head was beginning to ache from the turbid atmosphere.

"To meet with friends at a shop nearby."

"What kind of shop?"

"Oh, a place where coffins are made. We call ourselves the Eschatologists."

"Meaning what?"

"We share an interest in last things."

It didn't surprise me that Poe should have surrounded himself with men of a similarly morbid temperament. He was a man prowling the edges of society; even solitary persons will, however, gravitate to one another by the principle of mutual attraction. Edgar was devoted to his wife, Virginia, but I could not imagine her sharing in his dark fantasies. There was something of the ghoul in him.

"The Thanatopsis Club meets tonight," he said, and then he recited a mournful verse by William Cullen Bryant.

> Earth, that nourished thee, shall claim
> Thy growth, to be resolv'd to earth again;
> And, lost each human trace, surrend'ring up
> Thine individual being, shalt thou go
> To mix forever with the elements. . . .

Strange the things we remember!

"Life is short," said Poe. "What I can't abide is that it should not be ours." He cut a piece of sausage. "This bit at the end of my fork was once a pig that had its mud wallow, its apple parings, its muck, and never doubted—if pigs entertain doubt or hope—that its days would go on and on, one just like another. Then came the day when it was hauled up by block and tackle, its throat cut, and its leg used like a pump handle to empty it of blood. It's the same for us."

He chewed his meat and swallowed. The hairs of his mustache shone with grease.

I didn't know what to say, so I concentrated instead on a man sitting in the corner, whose nose had the purplish disfigurement known to medicine as rosacea. Here again, I thought, is a countenance marked like Cain's—the stigma of a pariah, which, if physiognomy has any truth to it, must have marked the man himself. My eyes welled up because of pity or, more likely, the tobacco smoke that made them smart. Choking on a piece of coarse black bread, Poe coughed alarmingly.

"Are you all right, Edgar?"

He emptied his glass of beer in a single draft, massaged his gullet, sputtered, and said, "Yes, thank you. It went down wrong."

We finished our supper without another word. Afterward, we walked east on Spring Garden to North Tenth and thence to Buttonwood, where, in an alleyway, we stopped before a carpenter's shop with a signboard reading: CABINET & COFFIN MAKERS. A black wreath hung on the door. The knocker, according to Poe, was a likeness of the hellhound Cerberus.

I NOTED THE HOUR AND THOUGHT to remind my visitor that it had grown late.

Moran, it's time you were leaving if you want to catch the last ferry to Philadelphia, unless the general will forgive your tardiness.

No, I wouldn't expect a general to wait, especially George Armstrong Custer. I've heard he's a vain and testy man. If you like and have time, you can come tomorrow and hear the rest of the story. It's worth a little inconvenience, I assure you. The climax is remarkable. What do you say, Moran?

Good! I'll expect you tomorrow, then.

PART TWO

. . . that it might so have happened that we
never had existed at all . . .

—Eureka, E. A. Poe

Camden, New Jersey, April 23, 1876

L ET'S HAVE THE WINDOW OPEN, Moran; the room is
warm this fine April morning. Have you had breakfast? What would you say to coffee and a piece of cake? The
woman who cleans for me makes the most delicious strudel.

No? If you should change your mind . . . I hope the general wasn't out of sorts last night.

Good.

To pick up the thread, it was the first night of February
1844. Having finished our supper, Poe and I went to a meeting of the Thanatopsis Club, held, from time to time, in a
carpenter's shop on Buttonwood Street. On the way there,
Edgar had told me how, in what he called "an excellent jest,"
he'd given each club member the name of an ancient god of
death. That night, I'd meet the Babylonian Nergal, the Etruscan Orcus, the Chinese Bao Zheng, the Japanese Shinigami,
the Egyptian Anubis, the Norse Odin, the Hindu Yama, the
African Ikú, and the Roman Mors. Poe had named himself
Thánatos, the personification of the death wish.

Edgar had told me, while we walked from Herr Schmidt's emporium of wurst, that the club was exclusive, its members drawn from the city's outcasts—that is, anyone connected in a professional capacity with death. I never knew whether the Thanatopsis Club was meant to be a serious convocation or an ironical one. Without doubt, it precipitated my downfall.

Philadelphia, February 1844

Edgar introduced me to that strange assembly as Mictlantecuhtli, the Aztec god whose symbols are the skull and the bloody skeleton, "suitable," said Poe with a poker face, "for the guardian of Death's anteroom."

His fellow actors in the indecent burlesque made a showy obeisance to the master.

"You may have noticed, Edward, that ordinary people have a distaste, even a disgust, for those who handle corpses or, in my case, write in an unseemly manner about them. You yourself must have seen people shy away from you as though you carried the plague."

I told him that I sensed a squeamishness in certain people when they learned that I worked for Dr. Mütter.

"You wear Mütter's 'pickling' agent like a rare perfume," said Poe with a smile.

I snuffled involuntarily at my shoulder.

"In the spring of last year, I decided to gather some of these pariahs—my work brings me into contact with the 'underworld'—into a coterie of specialists. I founded the Thanatopsis Club, if for no other reason than it affords us an opportunity and the privacy to discuss the business of our trades and, most important of all, to satisfy our addictions without fear of censure. We drink; we take ether; some of us 'eat the lotus' to our hearts' content. While we are in camera, we enjoy life in the midst of death—enjoy it all the more for death's dread warrants."

The workroom, which smelled wonderfully of freshly planed lumber, was decorated with memento mori: funereal crepe, sable ribbons, jet plumes worn by an undertaker's horse, a stuffed bird of ill omen, bizarre wall sconces fashioned of skulls, eye sockets fitted with candles, made even more cadaverous by an accumulation of wax over bone. The light shone dimly on a long table, set with bone china plates, an ironic touch of Edgar's, German cutlery whose handles bore a death's head, and pewter mugs inscribed with words from the *Dies Irae*: "*Requiem aeternam dona eis, Domine.*"

"Welcome to our merry little club!" Poe said, taking my coat and hat.

I was greeted pleasantly by Death's journeymen: a coroner; an embalmer, called by his fellow Eschatologists Anubis, the jackal-headed god of mummification; the dour hangman I'd seen send Rudolph Holtz, or Heinz, on his not-so-merry way; a negro grave digger, called Ikú in honor of his ancestors; a taxidermist; a morgue attendant; a professional mourner with a girlish face; a rat killer employed by the city; and a grizzled older man whose handiwork— "*petites maisons,*" Poe called the pine boxes—rested self-importantly on trestles, waiting for tenants.

"No shortage of customers in this town," the carpenter said with relish. "I can hardly keep up with demand."

"It's the times we live in," declared Orcus, the hairy bearded giant of the Etruscan netherworld, with a sigh.

The taxidermist and the hangman made room on the bench, and Edgar and I took our places at the table, presided over—so help me, Moran!—by a wickerwork mannequin dressed in widow's weeds.

"Drink up, gentlemen," said the embalmer, filling our mugs with bitter ale. "We have an hour's start on you."

I glanced at the clock, whose pendulum was unmoving and whose hands, stayed for all time, pointed to twelve—the midnight hour, of course.

"To your good health, Anubis!" said Edgar, raising his mug first to him and then to the other renegades sitting around the table. "And to all my friends in the jolly dance of death."

"I see that you've been admiring my raven," said the taxidermist named for Odin, who was known in Norse legends as the raven god. "I stuffed it in honor of our very own Thánatos." He bowed his bald head reverently to Poe. "To Thánatos!" he said, and drank.

"To Thánatos," his fellow ghouls cheered and did likewise.

"A clever fellow, your friend Mr. Poe," said the coroner, Yama, whose original had passed judgment on the Hindu dead. "If it weren't for him, we would be all alone in the world."

"Among gods, Thánatos is chief," said Nergal, the rat catcher, nibbling a piece of malodorous cheese.

In this fraternity of grim reapers, I sensed that the rat catcher was the lowliest; the men sitting to either side of him appeared to shrink from him, as if their sensibilities were offended by something other than overripe Stilton.

Poe was gracious in his acceptance of Nergal's compliment. He turned to Bao Zheng, renowned during the Song dynasty for his nimble execution of criminals, and said, "My friend Mictlantecuhtli, whose bloody namesake was feared even by the Aztecs, witnessed your last performance on the gibbet's little stage."

The sullen hangman glared at me as if expecting criticism. Intimidated, I mumbled some piece of flattery, which appeared to satisfy him.

"He is a prince among executioners," said Poe grandly. "If ever I must wear the hempen cravat, I can only hope it is our friend and companion who ties it."

"Here, here!" shouted the cabinet and coffin maker, the club's so-called Shinigami, who thumped the tabletop with the butt of his knife. Like most of the others present, he was on his way toward the little death of drunkenness that passed for the sacrament of Communion among them.

The androgynous mourner, Mors, a Roman god of death whom the Latin poets had idealized as feminine, stood up, staggered outside into the alleyway to vomit, and did not return.

"He has gone to keen over some poor soul," said Poe, who was, by now, also in his cups.

"Chances are I shall examine the remains in the morning," said Yama, the coroner.

"And you, master Ikú, shall bury him or her, for Death in his or her awful majesty does not discriminate between the sexes," said Poe.

"After I've boxed 'em up!" shouted the graying Shinigami, once again banging the table with his heavy knife, like a hungry man waiting for his meat.

Having been done out of the prospect of a fee by a draft of ether, Anubis, god of funerals, was whimpering in Duat, land of dead Egyptians, where his spirit had gone before him in search of corpses.

Most of the club's members had exchanged their mugs for glasses of ether, drunk neat, with a water chaser. Have you never heard of "ether frolics," Moran? They were in vogue in the 1840s, especially among Irish Catholics in order to satisfy the church's prohibition against strong drink. The result was identical: unconsciousness. Dr. Crawford Long, whom I knew slightly at the time, introduced it as an anesthetic to the pit of the University of Pennsylvania Hospital after having experienced it at a frolic. One man's poison is another man's balm.

Not to be unsociable, I tippled my portion of ether and woke—God save me from the memory—inside a coffin!

Imagine it, if you can, Moran: the cramped space, the wood squeezing your shoulders, the impossibility of raising your head or arms. Blackness darker than any night. The atmosphere, if you can call the thin air inside a coffin by so spacious a word, was compounded of the rank odors of sweat and of the lime pit where poxy corpses are thrown—thus it seemed to my feverish and overwrought imagination. While I struggled against the box, a part of me wished for—prayed for—quick annihilation, while another part screamed for help.

I fainted, only to awake instantly to the horror that,

moment by moment, increased. The anguish I felt, Moran—you'd have had to be buried alive, walled up, or shut away in a tomb to know its sharpness. My lips were parched; my tongue felt swollen in my mouth. I couldn't speak. I screamed for mercy's sake to be let out. I felt the blood run from under my broken nails, with which I'd tried to claw my way through the wooden lid. I'd have broken my teeth in gnawing if only I could have raised my head to bite at it. I was wet with the perspiration that starts from every pore when you're afraid, with the tears that will fill a man's eyes in desperation, with my own stale. I could scarcely breathe; I felt a weight upon my chest. I thought I must die; felt I could not survive a moment's longer. And then I heard the screech of iron nails as, one by one, they were clawed out with a hammer, and, in a moment, I saw the taxidermist's smooth face as he lifted the lid.

"Now you're one of us," he said, grinning like one of the room's waxen skulls, whose illumination was as feeble and uncertain as the light in hell.

He and the rat catcher helped me from the coffin. They had not taken ether, or else I would have been shut up still. The others were slumped at the table, their heads on their arms, profoundly insensible.

I stood on the rough-planked floor and shook uncontrollably, chilled by fear and my own urine-stained trousers. If I'd had Death's scythe, I would have laid waste to them all, awake or sleeping. I have never in my life known hatred equal to what I felt for those men. I cursed them.

"It was your initiation," said the rat catcher, smiling. "We all went through it. You were only in there a short while."

"We counted to a hundred and let you out," said the taxidermist, plunging his ear with a dirty finger.

One hundred! I tell you, Moran, it was an hour, a day, a week, an eternity that I spent inside the coffin. There is no measure of time to reckon the length of my imprisonment in that box that is worse than any jail or madhouse cell.

"You're a liar!" I stammered, in the grip of terror yet.

"I counted to a hundred and let you out," the man repeated stubbornly.

"True, true," said the rat catcher. He was leaning against a wall, and his arm and shoulder had vanished in shadow. "The same as for all of us."

"And *him*," I said, pointing to Edgar Poe, where he rested in tranquil oblivion at the table. "Did you count to a hundred for him?"

"No, he never did lie down inside the box. He's scared of tight places. He said he'd lose his wits if ever he was put inside a coffin and the lid nailed shut. Mr. Edgar's founder of our club. I guess we can made an exception for him."

"That's so," said the stuffer of birds and purveyor of ghastly souvenirs.

I shouted what used to be called "a soldier's oath," some vile obscenity, and wished that they, one and all, would perish on the spot. And then I left Poe to his ether dreams and hurried home to my mother's house like a child who has seen a ghost.

"You were unhappy last night at our little ceremony," said Edgar Poe—brazenly, I thought.

He stood in the doorway of the coop, like the angel Gabriel when he appeared to Mary in a radiant atmosphere, although—more fitting for a devil—the light, draped over Poe's narrow shoulders, was fouled by swirling dust and pigeon molt. I was still furious with him and his cohort. Had there been another door, I'd have walked through it and left him to consider how he had abused me. I looked him in the face and glared, afraid to speak in case I'd stammer again in fear. It would take time, Moran, to forget that night—longer than it took for my broken nails to grow. What am I saying? It would never be forgotten. I've only to ride past a graveyard or see a funeral in the street to remember those sensations. I've only to stand inside a dark closet and pull the door closed after me to begin to suffocate.

Poe reacted to my silent disdain with an uncommon show of humility. He shuffled his feet on the feed-strewn floor; he looked through the window at the tarred roofs across the street; he made a catarrhal noise in the back of his throat that might have been caused by dust but was more likely to be evidence of his embarrassment—at least that is how I chose to interpret it.

I broke my silence. "You've no idea of the terror your 'little ceremony' caused me."

"*Ahem.*" He made a noise as if to clear his throat or to introduce a theme that might upset me.

"You betrayed me!" I shouted, determined to nurse my grievance.

"I had no idea, Edward, that you would carry on so." He sounded as though he meant to belittle me. At that moment, I could have leaped at his throat. He saw the rage in my eyes and repented. "If I'd known of your aversion . . . I see that I overstepped the mark, Edward. You have my sincerest apologies. I see now that I presumed. Forgive me."

Earlier in the day, I'd told Dr. Mütter of what Poe and his ghouls had put me through. I'd trembled as I spoke; my hands had shaken as if with ague. My fear intrigued him. He took my pulse and temperature; he questioned me closely on my "symptoms": How had I behaved inside the coffin? Had my heart raced? Had I perspired? Had I felt hot or cold? Had my ears rung? Had I heard the sound of my blood sluicing in the chambers of my heart? He took down my answers. I was . . . annoyed. To be treated like a specimen angered me. But I dared not show it. He was my mentor; I was his protégé. My future depended on his goodwill and charitable disposition. I was ambitious, and I lacked the wherewithal to advance myself. I told him what he wanted to know. I may have even invented or embellished. In all honesty, my recollections of the night before were muddled. I could recount sensations; the experience itself was hardly recountable. Similes, figures of speech came more vividly to mind. But Mütter was no poet. Edgar Poe would write the tale, the thieving magpie.

"He's good for you, Edward, however much he appears to be the opposite," the doctor had said, fixing me with his gaze. "Anyone who has something to teach, to show you about life and death, is important to a doctor. I've seen you poring over our skulls. Admit they fascinate you, Edward." I nodded. "How then could a man like Edgar Poe fail to intrigue you, as well?"

I had agreed even though, at the time, I'd resented Poe and Mütter both.

Now, inside the coop, the pigeons were gossiping while they milled about the gritty floor, sometimes stopping to peck at our shoes. To think they possessed an intelligence was absurd.

"Forgive me," Poe repeated earnestly.

I nodded coldly. I was not above acting like a child; I was hardly more than one.

"I want you to have this," he said, fishing a gold watch and chain from his pocket. He took a step toward me. I stood my ground. He closed the distance between us, the timepiece in his hand. "It belonged to my father, David Poe—*not* John Allan, who fostered me but would not adopt me. My real father was David Poe, Jr., the actor. It's said that he abandoned my mother and me. It's a lie. He died— too young: He was only twenty-seven."

I accepted the gift. It felt substantial in my hand. In spite of myself, I was pleased to have it.

"Good," said Poe, having effected our truce. "When you tell the time, you will think of me, and, in time, I hope you'll forgive me."

This is the very watch and chain, Moran. Inside the lid, you can still make out the inscription:

> *To David From His "Eliza"*
> *September 1807*

"Thank you, Edgar. I'll treasure it."

I didn't mean it, but I've kept it with me all these years. Why, I'm not exactly sure. Not for love of Edgar Poe. I respected him; I admired him; I pitied him—perhaps that most of all. But I didn't love him and may not have even liked him. Dr. Mütter was right, however; Poe would fascinate me my entire life, and I do think it was important to have known him.

"It's the only thing I have of my father's," said Poe.

Looking back on it, I realize the full meaning of the gift: The watch and its heavy gold chain, in effect, bound him to his past, his paternity. To have given them to me was like cutting himself off from his original self. He was so very much a man adrift, cast off, and pushed to the margins of life, so that all that remained to him was an empty sheet of paper to fill up with words.

The pigeons scratched at the grit on the floor, making the sound of a pen on paper.

"I might have pawned it," said Poe about his gift to me, but I thought I owed you something for last night. Consider it a pledge of our friendship." He looked at the watch resting grandly on my palm with regret, as though he'd have liked to take it back.

"Thank you," I repeated while I scratched an itch on my cheek.

One night, while we were walking past a line of ships docked at the naval yard, Poe returned to my initiation into the afterlife—a rough sketch of what's to come.

"It's the fault of an unquenchable curiosity, which has been a burden and a curse since I was a boy. Without it, I couldn't write; because of it, I *must* write." He shrugged, unwilling to say which of the two punishments he preferred. Maybe he didn't know. He shrugged again and went on. "I couldn't help myself, Edward, although I was sufficiently distressed to hide in an ether-induced sleep." He paused and then admitted, "I find it hard to sleep in the ordinary way."

What a marvelous thing is sleep! Much more useful than Macbeth supposed when he praised its power to "knit up the ravell'd sleeve of care." It's a darkness in which to forget, to hide, and, for a time, to let the world go its way without you.

"I sleep like a log," I said to hurt him.

He looked at me with yearning, as though I were Morpheus, god of sleep, instead of the custodian of a charnel house. That's what I was, Moran. A caretaker of the dead. I hadn't the sense to know that I was no more exalted than the rat catcher or the negro grave digger, for all my fancy clothes.

"Tell me, Edward: What was it like to wake up in a coffin? I have to know, but the dread of confined spaces has prevented me from attempting the experiment. My fellow Eschatologists, I'm afraid, are too unimaginative to come back from death's threshold with anything like a story to tell. You can imagine what such dark knowledge would mean to a writer of horror tales."

"Didn't you dream it?" I asked mordantly. "Or were you too fuddled by ether to receive my mesmeric transmission from inside the coffin?" Never mind my screams, I thought, but did not say.

I could see the contest being waged within him: whether to grab the manure shovel hanging on the wall of the coop and cudgel my brains out or else to offer me some other bribe.

In the end, I told him what he wanted to know. Why should I have denied him access to my deepest emotions, my most private experience, to the secrets that I should have been allowed to take with me to the grave? Was he not the illustrious Edgar Allan Poe? Should his writer's curiosity have been left unsatisfied? Who was I to frustrate the desire of an eminent man of letters—or of medicine? I was a nobody, a protégé—not even that. I was Mr. Bones. I told Poe what he wanted to hear, just as I had told Dr. Mütter.

"The master of this ship is an acquaintance of mine," said Poe.

We'd halted on the naval yard dock before a two-masted brig, the USS *Grampus*. Poe hailed the second officer, who was on deck, lounging against a rail. The man recognized him and bid us come on board. We climbed the gangway and were escorted below to the captain's cabin.

"Whenever he's in port, he sends me word, and we drink a glass or two of rum in his cabin," said Poe as we descended the companionway. "He's been everywhere and knows a great many stories."

"Good evening, Edgar!" cried the captain, whose name was Simon Phillips. "I'm happy to see you. I hope you and Virginia are well."

"Well enough, Simon. I'd like you to be acquainted with my young friend here, Mr. Edward Fenzil, of this city."

The captain bowed with military courtesy, which made me ashamed not to be in uniform. America was at peace, momentarily. We would go to war with Mexico in two years' time, and I would put on an army captain's uniform in '63. In this country, one will always have his chance to play soldier and to die in earnest. By your one remaining eye, Moran, you yourself are nearly proof of that observation.

"Pleased to make your acquaintance, Mr. Fenzil," said the captain affably.

"No need to stand on ceremony," said Poe. "We're all friends here."

"So we are, Edgar. Edward, Edgar—a glass of the good Jamaican?"

"If you please," said Poe, rubbing his hands together briskly.

"Thank you, Simon," I said, blushing to my very roots to hear myself speak casually to the master of a United States ship of the line.

The captain was untroubled by my familiarity, but Poe smiled at me—sardonically, I thought.

We sipped the rum in silence. I felt its pleasant fire invade me, belly and limbs. I favor rye whiskey and like a glass of gin for the smell of juniper. But in my experience as a drinking man, there's nothing quite so gently warming as rum taken hot or as it comes from the bottle.

"I was telling Edward that you are a master storyteller," said Poe, leaching a trace of liquor from his mustache with his tongue.

The captain gave a self-deprecating laugh. "High praise indeed from one of the greatest of our living authors!"

Poe made a *tch*, *tch* sound meant to deflect the captain's compliment. I thought his show of modesty was less than sincere. I noted his always pale face had not colored in modesty.

"You may not know this, young man, but, last year, when I discovered that Edgar Allan Poe lived in Philadelphia, I sought him out when the *Grampus* was in dry-dock for repairs. He wrote my favorite sea story, *The Narrative of Arthur Gordon Pym of Nantucket*. Strange, isn't it, that the brig in that tale should have been named the *Grampus,* too?"

We drank to the strangeness of it.

"Tell us a story, Simon. It's a cold night worthy of a weird tale and a warming glass of rum."

Captain Phillips eased back in his chair and stretched his long legs toward the brazier. He searched his memory awhile, staring out the aft window toward the black river, where a steamer sowed bright sparks into the starless, moonless night. I admired the captain's gold-fringed epaulets and, on the desk, his naval hat, whose form suggested to me the very ship he commanded. The cabin smelled of Oriental tobacco, tar, cordage, lignite, and wet wool. The captain's cabin was a manly space, where great outcomes were bravely decided with aplomb.

I wondered what it would be like if I were to enlist in the navy. Then the ship creaked and lurched, and I recalled my fear of confinement and of climbing trees and ladders. However much I could picture myself strolling the quarterdeck, wearing a boat-shaped hat, I could not—for all the tea in China, as is said—imagine scampering barefoot up the ratlines or lying down, exhausted in every muscle and bone, in a berth no roomier than a coffin. There was more of the coward about me than the hero. In those days, I was often afraid. I knew my place: to submit to better men, to envy them the footlights and to lurk in the shadows of their eminence. Since then, I've distinguished myself in the field and have performed surgeries that required the steadiest of hands and nerves, but I'm still afraid.

You may wonder why I choose to make so unmanly an admission to you, a stranger. I'm usually reserved and circumspect. I've told only a few others this long and rambling story of my winter with Poe and never before have I betrayed my fears and weaknesses. But I like your face, Moran, and I sense in you someone who has not been altogether brave, in spite of your ferocious eye patch! I never got the chance to spoon out an eye during the war.

Aboard the *Grampus*, Phillips charged his briar pipe with tobacco imported, he said, from Anatolia. He'd first smoked it while on duty with the Africa Squadron, and he kept a supply in his cabin for special occasions.

"I'm pleased," said Poe, "that you count this rendezvous a special occasion. And now— Captain, if you please—a story to commemorate it."

Phillips glanced at his friend cordially while he drew on his pipe. I heard the tobacco crackle in the bowl, and we were soon engulfed in a heady cloud of smoke. His preparations completed, the captain leaned back in his chair again, tugged at his ear, and began his story.

"This excellent tobacco reminds me of a time three years ago when we sailed with the squadron. We'd departed New York for the Portuguese archipelago and had provisioned the ship in Madeira; thence we'd made for the west coast of Africa. We were charged with stopping any British or American vessel suspected of carrying slaves. We'd been out four months when we went aboard the United States merchant ship *Patuxent,* carrying sugarcane, according to her manifest. We found the cane and, down in the depths of the hold, a shipment of scared blacks. Her captain claimed they were 'blackbirds.'"

Do you know the term, Moran? It was used before the war by those who hoped to circumvent the prohibition on slave running by claiming that the Africans were 'blackberries,' meaning they were paid a wage and, therefore, were not slaves. It was a subterfuge employed by those who meant to steal, within the letter of the law, other human beings. Greedy, immoral men will always find a way to enrich themselves. I beg your pardon, Moran: High-mindedness is intolerable in anybody other than oneself.

"We boarded the *Patuxent* and took the Africans—men, women, and children—onto the *Grampus.* We fed and clothed them and, later, put them ashore at Cape Colony to fend for themselves. We could do no more. They'd come— God only knows the anguish of their capture—from up and down the coast and, many of them, from the interior. We could not entirely undo the injustice—feeble word—done them. We did, however, put the *Patuxent*'s master in chains.

"Sailing northerly toward Lisbon to resupply, the ship entered a fog bank like no other in my experience at sea. It seemed to have no end and was illumined by a peculiar glow such as that which torches make on mica at the bottom of a mine shaft or mashed fireflies leave on the palms of thoughtless children. After a time that might have been hours or days, so muddled were we all by—to call it 'fog,' gentlemen, is to give no true impression of its murk and obscurity."

Edgar's eyes had closed to rest, no doubt, on an inner vision.

"Finally, we came to the end of it, and the ship entered a zone unknown to me or to my officers. It reminded me— I'd made a study of arcane matters relating to my trade—of a Nubian geographer's account of Mare Tenebrarum, the name given to the Atlantic south of Morocco by fifteenth-century mariners. The Europeans and the Arabs believed it to be the southern limit of the world, a 'dark sea' impossible to cross. The Portuguese called the point of land that marked it Cabo de Não. The explorer Alvise Cadamosto wrote of that dark, wild ocean, '*Quem passar o Cabo de Não, ou tornará ou não*': 'Those who cross it will return or not.'

"But it was not Cape Não on our starboard beam, nor could the ocean have been Mare Tenebrarum, which the Arabs called Bahr al-Zulumat. We had been sailing in the nineteenth century, not the fifteenth. The world's seas and oceans had been charted. I myself had sailed the western coast of Africa many times, and yet, gentlemen, I could not recognize this bedeviled sea, which the wind blew into precipitous crags to make even the most able seamen afraid to go aloft to reef the sails. We plunged into warring currents like a toy boat and were swept with demonic speed around the rims of gigantic whirlpools. The noise terrified us, and we could not make ourselves heard above the din. I believed the ship would shortly founder and go down to the bottom of one of those gnashing maelstroms.

"Suddenly, a black man appeared to us on the water. In a moment, the wind had fallen, the ocean grown calm, and the shuddering *Grampus,* whose stern was buried by the sea, had righted and shaken off the foam from her sheets and rigging. He came striding across the slack water toward our ship, and, speaking through a grotesque mask in the language of the Yoruba, he demanded that we give up the *Patuxent*'s master. I don't know how we understood him, unless we were dreaming actors in what the Yoruba call Odun Egungun, a ceremony in which the Egun is possessed by one of his dead ancestors. We understood that this black man, standing tall and erect beside our hull, was, in fact, the slave who'd been beaten to death aboard the *Patuxent* for some 'insolence' to her master.

"I handed him over to the black. Why not? He was a brutal slave runner, deserving neither my protection nor my pity. Seamen are an unsentimental lot, Moran, and I was ship's captain, responsible for the lives of all aboard. I pushed the man over the side and watched him sink like a stone under the weight of his chains and his sins. The black man danced, briefly and ecstatically, and then he, too, sank beneath the flat calm of that most unnatural ocean."

The captain paused. Entranced by memory, he rubbed a thumb across the corner of his gray mustache. It rasped in the silence of the cabin. Edgar's eyes were still closed, and, for a moment, I wondered if he had gone to sleep. You could have heard the woodworms gnawing the bulkhead, so very quiet was it. The captain roused himself from his reverie and quickly finished his tale.

"Shortly, the natural currents reasserted themselves; the wind freshened and filled the sails, which, miraculously, had not been rent by the ferocious winds; and we were once again on course for Lisbon. The *Grampus* spanked along under a high, clear sky that held not even a memory of the dense fog that had enshrouded her. Having arrived in port, I polished my boots, donned my braided hat and finery, and went to see the admiral's man. I told him nothing about the weird sea or the black Jesus walking on the water. I reported that the *Patuxent*'s master had died en route of black water fever, common in the tropics. No one disputed my claim."

Was the captain's story the truth or a tall tale?

Moran, it doesn't matter.

Phillips drew on his pipe and sent another cloud of smoke into the roiling air. My mind a confusion of thoughts and fancies, I wondered if I had heard the story aright or if I'd imagined it, befuddled by rum and the strong Turkish tobacco. I glanced at Edgar, who seemed in a stupor. If not mine, was the tale his? Had it seeped into my mind from his unconsciousness through the pneuma of the smoky atmosphere? The tale was like one by Edgar Poe. In the years since then, I've read all of his stories to appear in print, but never have I come across one like that which I heard or dreamed aboard the *Grampus*.

We kept silent awhile, as people do who experience something beyond their power to assess. I looked out the stern window, as if I expected an Egun to be walking on the night-blackened Delaware. There was only the water and, moving slowly past our starboard side, a wooden crate, whose contents might have been anything you care to imagine: silks from Japan, opium from China, or a woman's head hacked off in a fit of jealous rage. By night, a river is a sluice for dark dreams . . . an artery feeding the bewildered hearts of men . . . a sewer. I left them to drink once more to the strangeness of life. I left the ship for the ice-cold air of a February night and walked, brooding over the captain's tale, to a sailors' taproom on Church Street, just beyond the naval yard.

At the bar, I stood beside an ordinary seaman arrived early that morning in Philadelphia after a cruise around the Horn. He'd been to Wake Island and the Philippines aboard the USS *Vincennes,* a Boston-class sloop of war, which had put into the yard for overhaul. I don't recall the man's name, though I told him mine—no, not mine, I'm embarrassed to admit. I told him my name was Edgar Poe. I haven't any excuse to make except that I was not myself at that late hour of the night. Like anyone who has drunk more than is good for him, I was eager to escape the confines of my narrow personality. Wishing to be somebody else, I took the first name that came to mind.

We drank until the barroom, with its maritime decorations and an amateur painting of the naval Battle of Plattsburg, began to gyre and the voices of the other inebriates grew distant. I remember the slap of coins on the bar, the scrape of my stool against the sawdust-strewn floor, the bang of a door, the sting on my face of the cold night air, an icy snuffle, and, outside a tattoo parlor, the hoarse voice of my friend—he was, by now, my boon companion, for whose sake I was prepared to martyr myself to drink—calling loudly through the shuttered window to be allowed inside. The proprietor must have let us in, for I awoke next morning on a broken couch in a corner of his shop with a painful arm and, beneath a scab, the tattoo of a rope looped around the inked words EDGAR POE.

I told you he had left an indelible stain on me. Here it is, Moran, the livid souvenir of that preposterous night. There is another, which you are kind to ignore. Have you ever in your life met a fool like me?

Yes? Well, you've knocked around the country long enough to have met a boatload of fools and madmen.

I got dressed and walked through the empty early-morning streets to the college, hoping to clean myself up before Mütter arrived. He was already there, however, and, creep as stealthily as I might, he found me out.

"Edward, you look as though you haven't been home to bed."

"Sorry, Dr. Mütter, I've been on the town," I mumbled sheepishly.

"With Edgar Poe, I suppose." His voice was neutral, calm; his eyes revealed nothing.

"Yes, sir. I've been observing him, as you suggested," I said, without, I hoped, a trace of irony.

"For your enlightenment," said Mütter.

I nodded soberly.

"There's blood on your shirt."

I had not wanted to tell him about my tattoo, but there was no help for it. He rolled up my sleeve and saw the evidence of my folly. He neither smiled nor frowned. When he spoke next, I couldn't tell whether he meant to chide me or encourage me. His tone was, if anything, clinical.

"Your empathy is exceptional, Edward, and I commend your dedication. It's dangerous to forget oneself, however; you must know who you are. And you must keep the wound clean until it's healed. I wouldn't want to see you in the pit, your gangrenous arm in the strap, waiting for my saw. Who would carry it to the incinerator afterward?"

I smiled wanly, feeling an exhaustion stealing over me. I had slept only a little, and that badly. And my damned arm hurt! Had I been alone, I would have cried in pity for myself. I was like someone who sees in the distance a wreck, the great waves washing over its ruined deck, soon to be seen no more. I couldn't see my life whole, couldn't see a future, and did not care to see what I was making of the present. My eyes were on the muddy toes of my shoes. I saw in them a token of my failure and my wretchedness. Well, Moran, I was sick with drink. Dr. Mütter knew I would be useless all the morning.

"You might as well go home and sleep," he said. "It's Saturday, in any case. I'll see you Monday morning."

"The pigeons," I said, remembering my avian subjects on the roof.

"I'll do it. I want to see how they're getting along."

I was grateful to him. The sight and smell of their guano—a green and oozing mess—would have brought me to my knees in a fit of vomiting. I rolled down my bloodied sleeve, put on my coat and hat, and left, wondering where Poe had spent the night.

ON THE WAY TO POE'S HOUSE, I stopped at a lunchroom on Spruce Street and made a breakfast of scrambled eggs and ham, chased with coffee so strong, I feared my spoon would melt. But it was what I needed, or at least my head did, which felt as if it were bound by a slowly tightening iron band. The ingenuity of the Inquisition has been matched only by our southern overseers and the modern surgeon, whose purpose is surely different but whose methods are much the same.

Did you ever see the "Pear of Anguish," Moran? It's a grim device of iron spikes, a spring, and a key. An instrument of torture, it's not far removed from the cervical dilator, the tonsil guillotine, or the hernia tool.

All this to say, I had a headache, the body's own chastisement for its abuse. While I sat contritely, eating for my body's good, a young medical student, whom I knew at the college, came into the lunchroom. Seeing me, he asked if he might share my table. My eyes indicated that he could. He did. He spoke his order to the man standing at the stove. He smiled at me in that exaggeratedly affable way of his, which always made me squirm.

"Good morning to you, Fenzil."

"Morning, Holloway."

"Nothing doing in the pit or at 'Madame Tussaud's'?"

He meant, of course, Dr. Mütter's museum.

"I've already been."

"Unwell, are you? I must say, Edward, you look like hell. If I were a gambling man, I'd wager you were out all night."

"I was," I said, unwilling to elaborate.

"I'm on my way home. I was on duty until seven o'clock this morning," he said self-importantly.

Unconcerned, I went on with my breakfast.

"You know we're all envious of you."

"Of me?" I said, surprised.

"Of your intimacy with the great man. We mere medical students are seldom honored with his confidences. You have the god's ear, Fenzil, and the god has yours." Holloway sighed like an acolyte or a lovesick girl. "Shame about Nathaniel Dickey. And after a brilliant piece of surgery, too! I tell you, Fenzil, we in the gallery were in awe of Mütter that afternoon."

I wiped the grease from my lips with a threadbare napkin and asked, "What about him?"

"Haven't you heard? The poor fellow did away with himself. I'm surprised you didn't know. Old Meigs said Mütter took it hard."

"He said nothing to me."

"No?"

Holloway's eyes shone to find out I was not so much in the doctor's confidence as he had supposed. He smiled in spite of himself and the sad news of Dickey's suicide. Holloway enjoyed childish pranks, like stuffing the fingers of my gloves with phalanx bones or putting a shaving mirror among a row of skulls, so that I'd wince to see my face among the faces of the dead when I went to dust them.

"Why would he do it?" I asked, shaken.

"Don't know," said Holloway, buttering his toast. "They fished his body out of the river yesterday. The color of a Maryland blue claw, he was. He looked as though the crabs had made a meal of him."

The students prided themselves on their gallows humor. I looked away in distaste.

Dr. Mütter never did mention Dickey to me, and I knew enough not to pry. I left Holloway to finish his breakfast. At the lunchroom door, I turned in time to see his wolfish smile.

Later, I asked Poe what could possibly have driven Dickey to take his own life.

"Before the operation," he said thoughtfully, "Dickey was a monster—a prodigy of nature, to be kind. He occupied a category of being all his own, like a gnome or troll—or the Minotaur, solitary on its island, at the center of its Labyrinth. Incomparable, Dickey may have been unmoved by others, their condemnation and disgust. He was a thing to be feared, in the same way as a creature out of myth is feared. Our fear of him gave him strength and a kind of arrogance."

Poe's fancy seemed absurd and insensitive. In my experience, artists show little respect for human suffering. They're too absorbed by their own creations. Somewhere he wrote, "*The pure Imagination* chooses, from *either Beauty or Deformity*.*" In the pages of a tale, one quality is like another: Both produce a single powerful effect on the imagination. Beauty or deformity—it was one and the same to him.

"The operation on his face made him merely ugly in the sight of others and in his own mind, as well," said Poe, touching his own. "By it, he forfeited his uniqueness, his sui generis condition. He could not stand to see the horror in the eyes of strangers or the pity in the eyes of those who may have loved him. God grant there was someone to love him! It may have been the look on his mother's face that sent him to the river. Mütter made him an ordinary man, and that's what did him in. The mind is a perilous swamp, Edward, worse than Bunyan's Slough of Despond, which refers only to the loss of faith. The loss of reason—now there is a subject for our time! There is no science to explain it adequately. My tales concern the mind breached and overwhelmed, but what is the anguish of literary characters to that of real men and women?"

He was not usually so honest about his art.

At a quarter to nine, I knocked at Poe's front door. Mrs. Clemm, hands red as boiled lobster, led me to the kitchen, where Edgar's shirts were, in fact, boiling on top of the stove. The room was pleasantly warm after my walk in the cold; the inside of its windows were dripping wet with steam.

"I must apologize, Mr. Fenzil," she said, "for receiving you in this unseemly way. But today is washing day, and our straitened circumstances oblige me to make economies. In other words, what I used to pay others to do, I now must do myself."

She sighed like one aggrieved who, nonetheless, takes pleasure in her martyrdom. I've known many, of both sexes, who delight in abasement: It bolsters their ego—a strange paradox.

She took a wooden paddle and stirred the steaming, soapy water. My nose stung a little because of the lye. She invited me to sit at the kitchen table and pour myself a cup of tea, if I were so inclined. I was not. My bladder was already incommoded, as Mütter used to say. I sat and watched her work, feeling a certain disdain, as though I were above such menial occupations. I was indulging a childish vanity, of course, for I did much worse than boil laundry: I got rid of bloody matter, rendered flesh from bone, and shoveled pigeon excrement. But that morning, I sat in the hot kitchen with the pleasing realization that I was a man at liberty who needn't exert himself until Monday morning.

"My nephew is asleep," she said. I thought I heard a mild reproof in her voice. But maybe not; perhaps I was the reproving one. Mrs. Clemm was devoted to her nephew and son-in-law. I have no doubt she believed in his greatness, if not in his abilities to earn an income for her daughter, Virginia. "He didn't come home last night until very late."

"How is Mrs. Poe?" I inquired politely.

"She's also asleep. I fear for her health, Mr. Fenzil. She is frail and delicate. She sleeps in the afternoons. The doctor says she has consumption. I hope it's not so." She fell silent, and then she asked, "Have you read my nephew's story 'Life in Death'?"

Moran, you may know it as "The Oval Portrait," the title Edgar later gave it.

"I haven't read it," I admitted.

She appeared to be shocked by my ignorance of her illustrious son-in-law and nephew's work.

"It is a remarkable tale," she said, putting down the paddle. "In it, a husband paints a portrait in oil of his youthful wife. He labors long and hard on it, and, while she sits day after day for him, she grows ever weaker, as if, with each brushstroke, he stole her vitality, giving it to the other woman in his life—she in his painting. When the picture is finished, the young wife is dead. I sometimes imagine that when Edgar has emptied his well—no genius is inexhaustible, Mr. Fenzil, not even his—when he has written his last word, my daughter will be dead, drained of life by his willfulness. I dare not protest; she adores him, and he her. I don't doubt it. But his love for 'the other woman' is too strong for Virginia to survive."

I said nothing. What could I say? Before I'd met Poe. I'd have thought her raving. But I knew him now—his animal magnetism—and, aware or not, how he could captivate and destroy.

I asked to be remembered to Virginia. I left no word for Edgar. I was certain that we'd see each other again before too long. There was a strange affinity between us, remember. I wore its scabby symbol on my arm. Something told me never to show him it.

"I'll see myself out, Mrs. Clemm," I said, leaving her to her laundry tub. "Good day to you."

Walking through the front room on my way to the door, I happened to see a manuscript written in Poe's awkward hand, lying on his desk. I had time to read the title of a new tale: "The Premature Burial."

AT THE END OF FEBRUARY, I attended a reading given by Edgar Poe of his newest work, which I'd seen in manuscript lying on his desk. I sat in the rear of the Walnut Street Theatre, pleased by its gilt and ornament, the gaslights providing an otherworldly atmosphere suitable for a gothic tale. Some two or two hundred and fifty persons had gathered on a bitterly cold night to hear Edgar's latest "research into the limits of experience," as I had heard him say about his work. What would Jefferson and Lafayette have made of his dismal fantasies? They'd been among the spectators of the theater's first production, in 1812, of *The Rivals*. This

evening's program promised "a tale of unrivaled horror &
dismay, the like of which has rarely been heard on the stage
of this or any other theatre." The fainthearted were advised
to leave before the start of Mr. Poe's reading. The price of
admission would be refunded without question. The screw
to our anxiety had been cleverly turned by the time Edgar
stepped into the footlights.

He wore his black frock coat—he owned no other—a
deep burgundy cravat, and a freshly laundered shirt, which,
doubtless, had been recently boiled in Mrs. Clemm's wash-
tub. His unruly hair had the sheen and blackness of a raven,
if you'll pardon an obvious simile; it was combed more carefully than was usual for him. Standing alone onstage, he
seemed a small, vulnerable man. But as he began to read,
raising his eyes from time to time to meet ours across the
gaslit footlights, I saw how sure he was of his work, if not of
himself. His voice was neither powerful nor weak; its peculiar intonation had little to do with Edgar's mildly southern
drawl. He spoke in a low register—I'd never known him to
raise it, not even in anger or excitement—that was beautifully modulated—musical, even. We hung on his every
word as he read "The Premature Burial." We made hardly
a sound while we listened raptly to the hideous story of a
man who believed himself coffined up and entombed while
in a cataleptic trance. I heard echoes of what I'd told Poe
concerning the horror of my own unnatural confinement
earlier that month.

I have it here, Moran. I have all his tales. Let me see. . . .
Here it is: "The Premature Burial," published in Philadelphia's *Dollar Newspaper*, in 1844. For a good many years, I

couldn't bring myself to think about it, much less read it. Now I can. I'm over the terror of that night when I suffered my own premature burial. I wonder that Poe didn't have me put into the coffin with a sheet of paper, a pencil, and a candle so that I might have written the tale myself. It is always this way for those of us who lack genius: We're made to serve them who possess it.

Here's the passage that finally drove me from the theater.

> I could not summon courage to move. I dared not make the effort which was to satisfy me of my fate—and yet there was something at my heart which whispered me it was sure. Despair—such as no other species of wretchedness ever calls into being—despair alone urged me, after long irresolution, to uplift the heavy lids of my eyes. I uplifted them. It was dark—all dark. I knew that the fit was over. I knew that the crisis of my disorder had long passed. I knew that I had now fully recovered the use of my visual faculties—and yet it was dark—all dark—the intense and utter raylessness of the Night that endureth for evermore.
>
> I endeavored to shriek—, and my lips and my parched tongue moved convulsively together in the attempt—but no voice issued from the cavernous lungs, which, oppressed as if by the weight of some incumbent mountain, gasped and palpitated, with the heart, at every elaborate and struggling inspiration.

I felt sweat dampen my face, my hair, my palms—the body's response to fear. Edgar continued to read his tale; its sentences gathered relentlessly toward an overwhelming outcome.

"The movement of the jaws, in this effort to cry aloud . . ."

To have my night at the Thanatopsis Club revived in me was more than I could bear. I left the theater before Edgar had reached the end of his story. As I hurried toward the door, I noticed Dr. Mütter and Mary. He was gazing at me in amusement.

I wanted company, Moran! I wanted to feel life—at least its phantom—move inside me. I didn't want to drink. Lately, I'd indulged too much and too often, and the alcohol induced in me a sensation nearer death—how I imagined it—than life. Only once before had I been with a woman; it had not gone well. But I hurried toward a woman now as a freezing man would a fire. I knew I would regret it afterward, but I rushed through the streets toward the house where my brother had taken me for my manly initiation, my trial by combat. The streets were fairly empty, with the cold and the hour, which was well past the close of the Saturday business day. I watched the breath come out of my mouth as if I were giving up the ghost.

Built in a style known as "Father, Son, and Holy Ghost" because of its three rooms, one atop another, the house stood near the corner of Dock and Carters streets. At that time of night, it lay in an unrelieved darkness conducive to plots and illicit meetings, criminal or amorous. The "visitors" to the house were mostly sailors, porters, road menders, and other laboring men. The three rooms smelled of carbolic soap, musk, stale tobacco, and sweat. The reek nauseated me, but I held down my rising gorge and followed a fat woman up the stairs. I didn't care to look closely at her face.

I remember a lumpy bed, the smudged chimney of a badly trimmed oil lamp, a stack of damp newspapers, the smell of an unemptied chamber pot. I will say this, Moran: The grossness of the scene drove all thoughts of burial from my mind. Terror had given way to numbness.

The woman spoke perfunctorily, as if she'd been hired to carry rubbish to the ash heap. I wished to find in my imagination a spark of affection, but it was quenched by actuality. There is no disillusion like that caused by a visit to a brothel. Her breast felt strange in my hand, like a lump of raw dough. Her hair was brittle, her mouth a gash that made me think of poor Nathaniel Dickey's ruined face. I toiled between her thighs until my mind's blankness became a screen on which a garish phantasmagoria appeared: By turns, I saw myself as Dickey, Poe, Mütter. By turns, the bawd beneath me became Virginia, Mary in her "Sally cap," and Ida. I watched in horror and in fascination while my varied selves clamped onto the bodies of these three virtuous women until I'd emptied myself of seed.

It was disconcerting, Moran, to say the least. The thought revolved in my mind: What might be the issue of this misspent night? A monster, a prodigy, or merely what a frightened young man can sire on the body of a whore? Combinations so wayward and perverse must, of necessity, produce an unholy outcome.

Listen to this, Moran; it's from one of the master's essays—"On Imagination," published in the 1849 issue of the *Southern Literary Messenger,* the year he died. I wish I could have been a fly on the wall to see if he received the dreadful visitor with a welcome or a whimper.

". . . the Imagination is unlimited. Its materials extend throughout the universe." Like the imponderable fluid! "Even out of deformities, it fabricates that *Beauty* which is at once its sole object and its inevitable test."

To imagine Beauty resulting from my having coupled with a prostitute is laughable! Had she a heart of gold (who can say she did not?), what seed would a man in my condition have sown? I was no better than she and, perhaps, a good deal worse. Edgar knew everything about literature and nothing about living men and women, who are not redeemed by the imagination as readily as its figments safely ensconced between the covers of a book.

I slunk away from the house of ill fame, ashamed for having pictured in my mind Poe's wife, Mütter's, and Ida, the chaste and inviolate. I thought nothing at all about the poor drab who had exchanged her body for a pocketful of coins. Generally, we don't give a damn about anyone, man or woman, whom circumstances have ruined. A whore is no better than she should be—so it was said by men and by women. In my time, Moran, I've seen a few on the mortuary slab, transformed by disease, drowning, or murder into something less than human.

Lying in my own bed, I couldn't sleep for thinking about what I'd done—no, not about what I'd *done,* but what'd I'd *imagined* doing. In the morning, shame still gnawing at a troubled conscience, I went to the German Reformed Church on Race Street, where Ida was a member of the congregation. I sat in a back pew and watched her shine in glory with the rest of the elect. I knew I would never be among them, would never taste God's mercy. According to Calvinism, as I understand it, to struggle against a nature conceived in "reprobation" is futile and pointless. God's grace is arbitrary, and those to whom it is withheld are damned. No surgeon, alchemist, or powerful juju can undo poor Adam's curse.

I soon became distracted and ceased to hear the niggling exhortations of a stout man wearing a Geneva gown who spoke for the Almighty of Days every Sunday morning at ten o'clock.

Do you know Poe's tale "The Imp of the Perverse"? It's a parable about compulsion. The narrator murders another man using a poisoned candle in a shut-up room and inherits the dead man's estate. Years later, he's struck by the thought that nothing stands in the way of his enjoyment of the fruits of his crime but his confession. Forthwith, he's seized, perversely, as if by an "invisible fiend," with an overmastering desire to confess. He does and is hanged. Sitting in church that Sunday, while sin and salvation played out their eternal drama—in High German—I was *made* to picture Virginia, Mary, and Ida ravished by four grotesques, one of them myself.

Ravished is a nice word found in sentimental novels. Between us, Moran, the word that stuck in my mind like shit to the bottom of a shoe was *fucked*. The thought of my having fucked, in the guise of Mütter, Poe, and Nathaniel Dickey, those three good women horrified me, but the more I entertained it, the more I could not let it go. If ever in His wildest imagination, God might have thought to show me mercy, I knew that, by silently intoning *fucked, fucked, fucked* in church while the choir lifted its voice a cappella in praise of Him, I'd blasted all hope of salvation.

"Forgive me, Ida!" I wanted to shout over the pious heads that separated us, amid the church's drab austerities.

After the recessional hymn, I waited across the street for Ida to come outside. When she did, she was surrounded by seraphim—or so I feverishly imagined. In actuality, they were three young women and a young man dressed in black. Each was clutching a black-bound copy of Holy Writ; each was breathing sanctity; each one seemed to float an inch or two above the dirty pavement. Unworthy, I turned my back on them. I had no idea where I ought to stand in the world: with the saints or the sinners. I liked neither faction. Where did Poe stand? Where did Mütter?

"EDWARD, I'M A DOCTOR and not a priest!" snarled Mütter. "Matters of the tormented soul are best left to churchmen—or to Edgar Poe and his acolytes."

I had been hinting at my guilty thoughts and wanted absolution. His and Mary's role in my nightmarish comedy, I kept to myself. I could not scrub my mind clean, Moran! The mind's morgue, where all repulsive thoughts are hidden, had opened wide and said "Amen."

"The physical world"—Mütter's glance swept its terrible reminders, preserved and neatly catalogued—"should be enough for you and any other would-be man of science!"

Ordinarily tranquil, he shook with anger over all

straitjackets of belief, causing kidney stones to rattle in the emesis basin in his hand. He strove to be brave and enlightened but was afraid that we were tied to God's apron strings by mesmerism. I think he hated the unseen and the imponderable.

Behind glass, the specimens, gross and inviolable, leered.

"You left before our friend had finished reading—left in a hurry," said Mütter. He had set the basin down and wished to change the subject. "I nearly followed you, but I couldn't decently leave Mary to suffer Poe's charnel fancies without an escort."

"I suddenly felt sick," I said, putting on a pitiable mask.

"Ah! Then your escape had nothing to do with the tale he had chosen to read us."

I couldn't tell if he meant to mock me or to console me.

"Not at all."

"It was a disturbing piece. I wouldn't have blamed you for leaving—not after the unpleasantness at the Thanatopsis Club. I could almost hear your story in his. It shook me, I don't mind telling you. It left me with a feeling of profound unease. I can't imagine what it must have meant for you to hear it."

What does he want with me? I asked myself. I nearly taunted him with Nathaniel Dickey's suicide, but I knew it was not in my interest to rub salt in the wound, if wound there was. He went on relentlessly.

"Did you go home?"

"I went to visit a whore," I said, to be vicious and adult.

He smiled again and said, "In your opinion was she satisfactory?"

I shrugged—forlornly, no doubt. I was unequal to his Monday-morning peevishness, whose cause, on this occasion, I couldn't imagine. Dr. Mütter could be cruel, like anyone who has charge over others—their living and their dying.

"Edward, I've been worried about you lately. I know I asked you to keep close to Mr. Poe for the furtherance of your knowledge of . . . the pathological mind, shall we say? The experience of knowing him ought to be enriching. But I begin to see the telltale marks of too great a strain on your psyche: the tattoo, your flight from the theater, your debauches. Now you boast of having visited a certain house. I'd hoped the association with him would begin to steel you to aspects of the world—a harsh and merciless place— you will increasingly encounter. A doctor must attempt the impossible: to get close to another human while keeping his distance. If you can't, Edward, you'll be destroyed like so many of Edgar Poe's characters are. Like the man himself will be one day. Mark my words, Edward: No good can come from such a life or such a mind as his."

"Should I keep clear of him?" I asked. Frightened, I meant the question sincerely.

"I'm afraid it's too late for that."

"Why is it too late?"

"The connection between you has grown too strong." He winked at me. "You're tied till death do you part. If Edgar's right and we carry on beyond the grave, not even that will separate you."

"Meaning?" I asked in vexation.

"Even a dead frog can be made to jump if its hind leg is connected to a galvanic battery."

Mütter liked to play the Sphinx.

We went up onto the roof. The east wind freshened, bringing with it the complex odors of tidal water, coal smoke from the steamers, fish and mussels on their way to the inevitable end of all things. In spite of my winter clothes, I trembled with cold.

"In the latest issue of *Chirurgical Journal*, I read an extract from a new book by Søren Kierkegaard, *Begrebet Angest*, which argues that the grant of inalienable freedom burdens us with choice. Obliged to choose and finding it difficult, we experience dread." I must have looked perplexed, because he continued with an illustration. "A man stands on the roof of a building like this one. Having come to the edge, he's afraid to fall, and, at the same time, he feels an urge to jump." Strange, that Poe should have used this example in one of his tales. "The tension produced by this harrowing choice Kierkegaard calls 'angst.' Do you feel anxious, Edward, standing at the edge?"

He must have mistaken my shivering for fear.

"No, I'm cold."

He looked amused. We went inside the coop and listened to the complaints of our diminutive subjects while they marched about the floor on the red twigs of their legs.

"What do you think, Edward? Are they also burdened by choice?" He nodded at the pigeons, which were chuckling over some secret. "No, I don't think so," he said, sadly answering his own question. "They don't choose to fly home; they just do. Whether it's at the behest of instinct, gravity, magnetism, or predestination, I don't know."

He had spoken almost brutally. Had his words been

knives, the coop would have resembled a bloody shambles. I think he knew even then that his search for a higher, sovereign faculty would fail.

"Poe's fictional characters remind me of our pigeons. They don't appear to choose, either. They're governed by something outside themselves. In 'William Wilson,' he wrote, '. . . I have been, in some measure, the slave of circumstances beyond human control.' I'd give a great deal to know why we do what we do."

We left the pigeons to themselves—to hatch their young or their conspiracies, to tune their harps or break their compass needles, to exult or to sharpen the tooth of nostalgia. In a show of bravado, I walked to the edge of the roof and stood there with my arms outstretched like a funambulist on the high wire, daring myself to fall or a raw wind to rise up and topple me or the God of the Calvinists to hurl me down onto the cobblestones amid swirling wraiths of snow. I waited for the galvanic battery to make me twitch!

"Is it to be the pit or the pendulum?" asked Mütter.

"I want to be someone else," I groaned.

Have you never felt it, Moran? That you wanted, for once, to defy fate, destiny, accident, or whatever it is that hunts us, even if it should mean destruction? Poe called it "perverseness." Of course, you have; it's written on your face.

"If you were a bird, Edward, you could jump and be upheld," said Mütter—kindly, I thought.

But I was not a bird, and I would fall.

Philadelphia, March 1844

In early March, I received an invitation from the Thanatopsis Club to meet two nights later at one of the city's morgues. You can see it on the wall, next to my diploma from Jefferson Medical College and a commendation from William Hammond, surgeon general of the Union army during the time of the great slaughter. I've saved the invitation to recall the exact day in which my wits were turned. Edgar enjoyed such jests as this funereal card, bordered in black, which he sent me in care of the college.

PRIVATE VIEWING

THE COMPANY OF MR. EDWARD FENZIL,

OF BATHTOWN, NORTHERN LIBERTIES,

IS REQUESTED AT THE MORGUE

ON CALLOWHILL STREET,

ON THURSDAY EVENING, MARCH 7, 1844,

AT 10 O'CLOCK.

THE THANATOPSIS CLUB

EDGAR A. POE, FOUNDER & PRESIDENT

I arrived at the appointed hour to find Edgar already there, together with Nergal, the rat catcher; Bao Zheng, the hangman; Yama, the coroner; and Orcus, the morgue attendant of the long beard and uncommon height. The latter greeted me as any host would a guest, although he did not offer to escort me through his damp domain, pointing out the novel appliances peculiar to his profession. He left the civilities to Edgar.

"I'm pleased you decided to join us, Mictlantecuhtli," he said.

Poe—remember—had named me after the god of the lowest Aztec hell, who'd worn a necklace of human eyes. Ironic, isn't it, Moran, in that you lost one of yours to Confederate shrapnel? I'd ask you to drink to the strangeness of life if it weren't too early in the morning even for reprobates to indulge.

"I nearly didn't come," I told him, smarting still at the memory of my initiation into the rites and mysteries of the end of time that arrives to each and every one of us, a rehearsal for the harrowing last act of the play called *Man*. But, like a man who puts on a suit of armor and leaves the safety of the castle walls, I'd fortified myself and gone into the midst of my enemies to show them I was unafraid.

Did I think of Edgar Poe as an enemy?

An enemy one becomes captivated by, perhaps.

Damn it, Moran! I think we *should* make a libation. What will you have? Rye, gin, rum, or stout, which is the most nourishing of the four sacred tipples.

Stout it is! Mind the foam. To the strangeness of life and the confounding of Death in all its grim guises!

Let us return to the dread precincts of Death, the morgue, whose smell I recall in the sharp stinging in my nostrils produced by this blessed concoction of grain, hops, and yeast. You remember the smell, Moran. "Death's bouquet," we called it. You were in the Armory Square Hospital, where Whitman nursed his boys. Let's drink to the "wound dresser" and Good Gray Poet!

The morgue was subject to a "creeping damp"; in a short

while, the chill of it had invaded the marrow of my bones. I would have liked nothing more than to rush out into the street, which, wet and cold with an early-March rain, was still less miserable than this. Even now, the memory makes me think of "The Cask of Amontillado," Edgar's tale of entombment in the catacombs of the Montresors, gleaming phantasmagorically with niter. I coughed just as poor Fortunato had done as he was goaded by deceit and his own base appetite down the stone steps to the chains that had been prepared to receive him. This was not one of the "waiting mortuaries" favored by the Germans, where the deceased's body is laid, with a bell pull tied around its wrist, until decomposition should settle the question of its death. The Callowhill morgue was the anteroom of the grave, sharing in its dankness, mold, and penetrating chill. With the gaslights licking the stone walls, I might as easily have called it "hell's vestibule." Faint of heart, I was determined to keep my uneasiness from the fraternity of ghouls. Several bottles of "embalming fluid" kept them warm and sociable. I was relieved that no one had brought the ether bottle; a combustible in that close space would have put us all to sleep or blown us to kingdom come.

"In English, the French word *morgue* means 'to look at defiantly,'" said Edgar, swaggering like a music hall impresario. "We are, all of us, equal to the meaning of the word. A test of nerves, however, is not the reason we are gathered here tonight. Mr. Buffone—pardon me . . . *Orcus,* warder of this dismal establishment, has made a discovery of vital interest to our newest member. Edward, I recommend fortification before brother Orcus proceeds."

Poe's roundabout prologue was beginning to anger me. I glared at him, but he had taken his own advice and was throwing a glass of gin down his gullet. He smacked his mustached lips, wiped them on the back of his hand, and then went on as before.

"Two days ago, in the Southwark district of our fair city, a man, after having murdered a shopkeeper, was shot dead by a constable. The deceased was thrown into a Black Maria and unceremoniously transported here to await claimants. None has stepped forward, doubtless ashamed to admit a familial connection to a strangler, and the body, therefore, will shortly be put to bed in a pauper's grave, there to begin the death sentence administered by Conqueror Worm. Orcus, an astute fellow, noticed—was it immediately?" Orcus nodded. "Orcus noticed *immediately* that the corpse bore—"

Poe had stopped in mid-sentence to enhance the suspense. I felt as the hanged man must have when he made his slow, final voyage toward the ground beneath the gibbet.

"What're you trying to say, Edgar!" I shouted, loudly enough for me to hear my impatience echo from the damp walls.

He waved his hand in the direction of the mortuary attendant, who, with the flourish of an artist about to unveil a new sculpture, whisked a white sheet from a cadaver that had been lying unnoticed among the city's recently departed. You can't begin to imagine the horror with which I beheld, lying on a slab, a dead man who was the very image of myself.

"Behold the doppelgänger!" Poe shouted in a weirdly

ecstatic voice, as if the secret of the universe were to be seen lying on the stone and not the withering remains of my dead facsimile.

I don't know what dramatic effect Poe intended to produce by this dumb show, whether horror or religious awe. His "untouchables" were halted in whatever they were about to do: drink another draft of liquor, mostly, their mouths opened, revealing missing or bad teeth. They were silenced; all of us were, for the moment, silenced, even the pantomime's author and his collaborator, Buffone. I thought I heard the sound of water dripping onto stone, but it might have been only in my mind that it fell. Someone coughed—it could have been I who coughed—and we were brought back with a jolt to the contemplation of my dead twin. We were alike in every particular except for a port-wine stain on his cheek.

"Damn me, if he's not the spitting image of Edward!" the coroner cried enthusiastically.

His opinion in matters of mortality was considered to be authoritative; he had the last word on the subject.

"He is *that*!" The rat catcher sniggered for a reason best known to outcasts who bore the peculiar stink of their repulsive trade.

Poe nodded toward the attendant, who produced a camera and tripod from another room.

"Stand the fellow up!" commanded Poe, and our burly hangman raised the dead body to its feet. "Stand beside your doppelgänger," Poe said to me in a voice that could not be gainsaid.

I stood next to my dead other—my blood turned cold in my veins, like his—and, after having turned the gaslights

up to flood the room with a garish and an unnatural bril-
liance, Orcus began to fumble with the lens.

"Stand still!" he ordered.

In that my double would never move again of his own
volition, I knew he meant me.

"Now don't move a muscle until I've counted to fifty."

I assumed a pose as rigid as my twin's while Edgar
rubbed his hands gleefully, like a boy who has just smoked
out a nest of wasps.

". . . forty-eight, forty-nine, fifty," said Orcus, covering
the camera's lens.

Had the earth vomited instead of me, trees would have
been uprooted and mountains torn from its bowels. As I'd
done after my premature burial, I rushed out into the street,
determined to put as much distance between my other self
and me as I could that night.

I paused in my homeward flight outside the city's House
of Refuge and leaned against its rough stone wall to catch
my breath.

"Take my hand," a shadow adjured me—not a shadow,
but a man standing in one.

He stumbled toward me with his hand outstretched.
He was an old man, even an ancient one, dressed bizarrely
like a character in a Washington Irving tale: a pigtail tied
with a ribbon, a tricornered hat, an antique cloak, an old-
fashioned frock coat, knee breeches, and buckled shoes.
In spite of myself and my recent shock, I laughed at the
strangeness of the apparition. He was not insulted. Perhaps
he hadn't noticed my derision. He repeated that I should
take his hand. I did and felt a thing as dry and bony as a

stick. I flinched and would have taken back my hand, but he held it fast in his own.

"When I was a boy," he said in a distant, quavering voice, "I saw General Washington ride down Market Street on his white horse, Nelson. I saw Ben Franklin on his way to the Grand Convention. I heard the bells ring for the reading of the Declaration of Independence. All that is in me from those days is now in you. Memory is electric, like what's stored in the brass ball of Franklin's electrostatic machine, waiting for its spark to jump from one mind into another's."

Holding his hand, I thought I had felt the spark.

He let go of mine and looked at me curiously. "They say I'm mad," he said.

He stepped back into his shadow and was gone—to Sleepy Hollow, perchance, to dream some more.

I WAS FINISHED WITH POE and resolved not to see him again, even if it should cost me Dr. Mütter's patronage. Two or three weeks had passed, and I began to feel safe from him and his baleful influence, when, while dusting the skulls on the shelf, I happened to see my own—that is, my twin's. Striking out wildly, I broke a jar in which a fetus had been swimming; it slipped out and came to rest in a puddle on the floor. I was beside myself! Wouldn't you have felt the same, Moran, to see yourself rendered down to bone, grinning back at you? I must have shouted in dismay, because Mütter came hurrying into the exhibits room, a dissecting scalpel in his hand.

"What is it, Edward?" he asked, and, in spite of my consternation, I was pleased to hear a genuine concern beneath his gruffness.

Speechless as the skulls themselves, I pointed to my doppelgänger's. Clenched between its teeth—the slack jaw bandaged shut—was a paper inscribed in India ink with these words:

EDWARD A. FENZIL
BORN DECEMBER 29, 1824
DIED MARCH 5, 1844

Mütter laughed. I suppose to him the joke was irresistible. "It's a student prank, Edward. In the worst of taste, of course, but our young men are a rowdy, childish lot. I shouldn't let it distress you."

"You don't understand," I said, tremors passing through me like an electric current.

"What don't I understand?" asked Mütter.

"It's my skull bone sitting on the shelf—or it might as well be."

Then I told him the story of the encounter with my doppelgänger in the Callowhill morgue, my gaze fixed in fascination on a drop of blood resisting gravity at the edge of Mütter's scalpel. While I spoke, there was in me a voice that asked to know what kind of blood it was. A rat's? A dog's? A pigeon's? Or was it human blood? One looks like another to the naked eye. I suppose it's only from the quantity of blood—its profusion—that we can guess its source without benefit of a body. My mother had been surprised when a colored boy, son of a stable hand, had cut his finger on broken glass. Friends, we'd been throwing stones at empty bottles. Later, she said that she would never have guessed a black person's blood could be red like ours.

When I'd finished my panicked recitation, Mütter replied with a reasonableness meant to comfort me. "The light in the morgue is treacherous, Edward, and you may, in fact, have borne only slight resemblance to the dead man."

His composure enraged me, for I had lost mine completely.

"From what you've told me, your friends are not above playing a practical joke, either. With rouge and chalk, an embalmer could produce the desired effect in that starkly lighted place where one might almost expect to see ghosts. Smartly done by an able man, the illusion could have persuaded a far less susceptible person than you of its reality."

"I looked exactly like him," I said doggedly. "He looked exactly like me. We looked exactly like each other except for the blemish on his cheek."

"Let me grant you, then, that you did see your double." He was all patience and reason. "What of it? While the chances are slight, the encounter is not impossible. I don't doubt that there exists, for some of us anyway, a likeness that may even, in rare instances, be perfect. The world is large, and there are a great many people in it. Doppelgängers may be among them. I further grant you that to meet one's own in a morgue, at night, in such fantastical company would be terrifying. But the encounter does not signify that your life is at risk either from harm or damnation. There may be doppelgängers, but Poe's use of the idea in 'William Wilson' is absurd. He based his tale on an impossibly evolved affinity where to kill one's double is to kill oneself. It's laughable!"

I did not laugh, but I thought it best to pretend to Dr. Mütter that his logic had convinced me of my childishness. Satisfied as much with himself as with me, he returned to the dissecting room, while I went to the pit to observe Dr. Chapman operate on an ulcerated artery after a second hemorrhaging brought on by a night of "excess," meaning whiskey and women. The patient, an ironmonger, had been shot six days earlier and, having had the wound dressed by a barber-surgeon, never realized that his earthly vessel would shortly be unstoppered and his life's blood let to spill onto the floor. I did not see him go. I was preoccupied by the mortal danger in which I found myself—and would soon lose myself. When the corpse had been removed, I went into the pit and mopped. Watching the red strings of the mop turn the water in the pail to blood, I thought of old Aaron's parlor trick.

By the afternoon, I had almost forgotten my doppelgänger when, having taken the specimen book from the shelf in order to catalogue a prodigious gallstone, I happened to turn to the osteological pages and saw my name and entry written there:

Name, age: Edward Arthur Fenzil, 19
Gender: Male
Place of Origin: Philadelphia, Pennsylvania
Cause of Death: Delirium tremens and moral
    degeneracy
Description: Port-wine stain on cheek. Warder of
    Mütter's monsters

Holloway! No one else would have carried the joke, if joke it was meant to be, to this extreme. Enraged, I went in search of him. At that moment, I wouldn't have cared if Dr. Mütter had come into the room with George Washington's brain on a tray to be pickled and catalogued. Goddamn Holloway! I could have filleted him with the nearest scalpel. I found him sitting in a quiet corner of the medical library, smoking a cheroot.

"Goddamn you!" I shouted in his face, whose mouth, after the cigar had been removed, relaxed into a grin.

"What is it now, Fenzil? Has one of your skeletal exhibits run off?"

I hit him. I saw the blood come out on his upper lip, soaking a portion of his dandified mustache. I saw him remove a white handkerchief from his pocket and daub at it. The blood—so crimson!—made a rose-shaped stain on the linen. A small gray rose of ash had fallen from the end of his cigar. My anger spent, I was suddenly calm.

"You oughtn't to have done that, you know," he said.

For a moment, I thought he meant to slap my cheek and challenge me to a duel: scalpels at twenty paces, lancets at dawn. But he was too taken aback and much too craven for charades.

"Where did you get it, Holloway?"

He knew what I meant. "A friend sent it over last night while I was on duty."

"What friend?"

"Buffone, the hairy attendant."

I was surprised that he would know such a person.

"I make it a point to cultivate friends in low places,"

he said smugly. "I don't expect to have a brilliant career doctoring, Fenzil. I'm just a muddler. If I didn't have a few good friends in *high* places—or, rather, if my father didn't—I wouldn't be enrolled here at all. Father has his heart set on my following in his footsteps. To be frank, mine isn't in it. I'm sure to botch things once in a while, and I wouldn't want my ineptitude becoming common knowledge. You know what they say: Dead men tell no tales, but the coroner, the mortician, and the morgue chap will unless you're on good terms with them. You might say I'm an honorary Eschatologist." He laughed, delighted with himself. "They appreciate the occasional gift of a bottle—doesn't matter what so long as it scalds the inner man. Now if you'll forgive me, Fenzil, I need an astringent and a sticking plaster."

"Then you know Edgar Poe?" I asked as he removed his bulk from the depths of the chair with a creak of leather.

"Everybody in the 'underworld' knows Thánatos."

"Did he put Buffone up to it?"

Holloway shrugged and said, "You have to find that out for yourself."

He left me alone in the room, with only the ghost of his tobacco smoke to mark his having been there.

Holloway died this year. His heart. He grew to be enormously fat! He was also in the gallery when Eakins made his preliminary sketches for *Dr. Gross's Clinic*. I was pleased to no end when I saw that Holloway had been left out of the final painting.

"Revenge, revenge," Timotheus cries,
"See the furies arise,
See the snakes that they rear,
How they hiss in their hair,
And the sparkles that flash from their eyes!"

Sorry, Moran, I've not much of a singing voice. But Handel knew the delicious meal that malice sometimes makes.

That night, I returned to the morgue to confront Buffone. The negro grave digger was with him. They were sharing a bottle of Old Tom gin without bothering to wipe its mouth on their sleeves. I always thought that drunkards were the true democrats.

Buffone set the bottle down on an empty slab and shouted, "Mictlantecuhtli!"

"My name is Fenzil," I said. My scowl went unnoticed where faces of pain, fear, regret, and protest were commonplace.

"Mr. *Fenzil*, please forgive me," he said, bowing genteelly in an alcoholic befuddlement. "You are correct inasmuch as the Thanatopsis Club has not been called into session. Having put aside, for the moment, our divine natures, we are met here tonight as ordinary friends."

"I'm not your friend."

"No? Acquaintances, then. We are acquaintances—there's no disputing the fact. Am I right, Young Werther?" he asked the negro. "He was named thus by his ol' *massa* for his sorrows. His *massa* was a southern gentleman who taught the classics of literature to little southern *massas* and gents in English, German, French, and, if I'm not

mistaken, Greek. My friend has sorrowed a great deal.
You've sorrowed a great deal, haven't you, Young Werther?
Sorrowed and suffered."

The grave digger indicated that he had sorrowed and
suffered.

"He's no longer young, of course. His sorrows have aged
him, turned his woolly pate white. White like the hair of
a southern gentleman at a dignified time of life." Buffone
took another drink from the gin bottle and then thought
to offer me some. I declined. "What do you want here?" he
asked, his tone sharpened by my look of distaste.

"Why did you send Holloway my double's skull?"

"Did it disturb you?" he asked silkily.

"It did. Why did you send it?" I hoped I sounded righ-
teously indignant, but I probably sounded fretful, like a
sulking child. "Did Edgar Poe put you up to it?"

"He did. He thought you would enjoy having—what did
he say? He thought you'd enjoy having your very own Yor-
rick to talk to. Isn't that right, Young Werther?"

The grave digger nodded. Having never once heard him
speak, I wondered if he were a mute.

"Are you familiar with the Bard's greatest work, *The
Tragedy of Hamlet, Prince of Denmark*? There's a grave digger in it. Two, in fact. Isn't that right, Young Werther?
More than once, I've read the play from beginning to end
for my friend here. Helps to pass the long nights in the
tomb. He keeps me company—don't you keep me company, Young Werther?"

Once again, the negro nodded his head.

"We pass the long nights together, drinking, reading,

reciting from the classics. People shy from us. They say we stink of death. Maybe we do, though I can't say I smell anything out of the ordinary. Young Werther and I think that the graveyard scene in *Hamlet* is the best of all. 'There is no ancient gentleman but gardeners, ditchers, and grave-makers: they hold up Adam's profession.' Old Will called his two grave diggers 'clowns,' which was a rude remark. Young Werther is no clown; he has the dignity of his sorrows to elevate him above most of them he plants. He got his tongue cut out for having the gall to ask his *ol' massa* not to sell his wife."

The speechless grave digger drank deeply from the bottle, as if in honor of himself.

"And to pay him back in kind, and a little more, Young Werther stove his *ol' massa's* head in with a shovel. And don't you know that, after a terrifying journey to freedom through malarial swamps and towns dark with ancient anger, the Good Lord put a shovel in his hands and bid him dig graves? Mysterious are the ways of the Lord—mysterious and cunning!"

Young Werther drank deeply to the perplexities of life and death.

NEXT MORNING, ITS BEING SATURDAY, I went to Edgar's house to have it out with him. A middle-aged colored woman answered my knock on the front door. She eyed me suspiciously. I suppose I gave a fairly good impression of a man with a grievance. I told her I wanted to see Mr. Poe.

"He ain't home," she said curtly, beginning to close the door on me.

"Who is it, Aunt Sarah?" It was Virginia's voice arriving faint and small from inside the house.

"It's Edward Fenzil, Mrs. Poe," I called. "Edgar's friend." I could be a plausible and fraudulent young man.

"Come in, Mr. Fenzil. Let the gentleman in, Sarah."

Sarah grunted and let me pass.

Virginia was lying on the sofa, a tartan blanket covering her. The fire had been made up in the grate, but the room was damp on that March morning. Gloomy and chill, the house might have been decorated by Poe himself in a style suitable to his tales. Virginia made an effort to rise in order to greet me but sank once more into lassitude. I wondered if I ought to go to her and kiss her hand. In those days, I knew nothing of propriety. Not that I'm a hand kisser now, but I know enough to attend a sickbed in a rich man's house.

"Don't get up," I said, in lieu of anything decorous.

She smiled at me—gratefully, I thought.

"Edgar's not at home," she said. "He's visiting Mr. Lowell." James Russell Lowell was, at the time, editing an abolitionist newspaper in Philadelphia. "My mother is at the stores. Aunt Sarah used to do our washing, and she's kind enough to sit with me when I'd be alone otherwise."

Virginia lay on the sofa, weak and forlorn, and I forgot my anger. Despite her illness, she was pretty, and not much older than I. Seeing her pallor and listlessness, I felt foolish. I'd seen my dead twin; I'd handled his skull. What of it? My complaint was trivial. She closed her eyes; the lids were nearly transparent. She was so young, Moran! I wondered what their life together was like, hers and Edgar's. I could not picture intimacy. She was frail and otherworldly, while Poe was ensorcelled by his own phantasms.

"Edgar is busy with his writing," she said apologetically, to account for his absence. "He often visits Mr. Lowell, who understands it."

"What do you think of it?" I asked, to have something to say.

"I think what the world thinks: That it is fine, although I confess, Mr. Fenzil, that I don't read it. It's too sensational; my nerves won't stand for it."

She was like a child. But I couldn't imagine Poe as her father any more than I could as her husband. Brother and sister, then. She was his Sis, after all, his Sissie. There was in him something that defied categorization. He was an original. Maybe that's what it means to possess genius. He and Virginia must have passed their days and nights together, chastely, in the rarefied atmosphere of a sentimental novel. If he looked at her—he must have sometimes looked at her—it was not with desire, but with curiosity. I could picture him reading poetry to her—not his own—and her, at the piano, singing and playing "The Blue Juniata," "The May Queen," or "Sleeping, I Dreamed of Love." She had done so up until two years before, when she'd broken a blood vessel in her throat. That was the beginning of her long illness. The piano was gone—sold, no doubt, to pay a debt. They would never, in their short lives, be free of financial crises and panics.

"Will you have tea, Mr. Fenzil?" she asked. "Sarah will bring it if you like."

"No, thank you. I have to go. An appointment."

"So soon?"

She looked relieved. I suppose she wanted to shut her eyes again.

"Don't get up, Mrs. Poe. I'll let myself out."

"I'll tell Edgar you paid us a visit. He'll be disappointed to have missed you."

I nodded, smiled, and moved toward the door. My gaze fell on a stack of writing paper on Poe's desk. A new story—*one dedicated to me*! I looked at Virginia; her eyes were closed; and, hesitating hardly at all, I purloined the manuscript. On the desk, a tintype of my dead other, reunited with me, glared from under glass, inside a frame of yellowed ivory. The smudge of his—or its—disfigurement was just visible on the cheek.

At home that evening, I sat by the fire while my mother sewed and gabbled as inconsequentially as the pigeons in Mütter's coop. She insisted on recounting the minutia of her day: what the butcher had said to her and how she'd answered him; how she'd nearly turned an ankle on the front step, whose bricks needed pointing; the state of poor Mrs. Murphy's lumbago and Mr. Crowther's gout; the saucy color of Anne-Marie's wool stockings poking out from the skirt of her dress for all the world to see. And then there were the questions: When did I think my brother, Franklin, would come home and in what condition would he drag himself upstairs to bed? Had I been to see Ida lately, and did I care any for her? Did it snow last year this time, or was she thinking of the year before? What was I reading? If I weren't careful, I'd end up looking through spectacles. She took hers off and rubbed the indentations on either side of her nose.

"I ruined my eyes to keep a roof over our heads and food on the table," she grumbled.

I nodded without taking mine from the manuscript.

"What is that you've got on your lap, Edward?" she said, putting her sewing on hers.

"It's a new story by Edgar Poe."

"I don't like you going around with that man," she complained. "I do believe he's a worse influence than the men your brother associates with, and the Lord knows what shiftless idlers and roughnecks they are. Miss Paulson, who is so *very* refined and plays the organ at First Methodist, says Poe's stories are scandalous and unfit to be in a Christian house. For God's sake, Edward, burn it on the grate and shame the devil! On second thought, it probably contains enough foul wickedness to call up the devil in the smoke. I don't know what you see in him to admire, Edward!"

I kept quiet, knowing that her indignation would soon sputter and go out.

"Well, if you're going to sit there and read all night, I might as well go to bed before your brother comes home and upsets the furniture."

She folded the sewing—a little white First Communion dress—and, having put it in her basket, she went upstairs.

After she'd shut the bedroom door behind her, my ears rang as silence was abruptly restored to the house. Not having grasped the pages that I'd tried to read during her nattering, I turned to the beginning of the manuscript and began again.

The Port-Wine Stain;

A Tale by Edgar A. Poe

For E. A. Fenzil

For I do not agree with those who have recently
begun to argue that soul and body perish at the
same time, and that all things are destroyed by
death.

—Cicero, *Laelius de Amicitia*

A man is bound to his double, even should he
never learn of its existence, by the umbilical of
an ancient grudge.

—Sir Launcelot Canning, *The Mad Trist*

I

~~In the City of London, at that gallery famous for its lifelike~~
~~grotesques, Edward F———, a resident of Philadelphia,~~
~~beheld his visage in the waxen face of a murderer.~~

[Poe struck out that first sentence and began his
tale anew.]

In London, at that gallery famous for its lifelike grotesques in
wax, I saw my face reflected—as it might have been by a mirror into which I had casually glanced—by the face of a murderer. I had arrived in that ancient city, three days earlier, from
Philadelphia, where I was, by profession, a teacher of ethics
at one of its universities. My purpose in coming to London
was to read *Super Ethica,* by Albertus Magnus, in the *Opera*

Omnia edition, published in Lyon in 1651, and, at the time of my visit, residing in the rare book collection of the British Library. My first transatlantic crossing was to have been a pilgrimage, in that this supreme work of moral philosophy had long been a touchstone (if I may be permitted an allusion to Magnus's alchemical studies) of the philosophical literature of friendship. I was interested, especially, in his notion of the *consensiom*, the movement within the human spirit that produces, like a sympathetic vibration, a harmony between things divine and human. It is the moral goodness that Cicero believed to be the very essence of friendship.*

[Poe added a footnote here, stating, "Magnus affirmed three types of friendship: the first is founded on usefulness (*amicitia utilis*), the second on pleasure (*amicitia delectabilis*), the third and finest on unqualified goodness (*amicitia honesti, amicitia quae fundatur super honestum*)." The tale continues.]

Earlier in my career, I had been struck by the similarity of Magnus's *consensiom* and Mesmer's notion of an "imponderable fluid," which transmits influences among beings and objects in the universe. By this ethereal machinery, angels inspire men and devils incite them, the moon affects the tides and the womb and the brain the movement of the hand. And by its invisible workings, two persons are conjoined in that most perfect of harmonies: friendship. Logically, the inverse must also be the case: *Disharmony* will produce enmity transmitted by Mesmer's fluid, which is everywhere present in the universe, including the microcosm that is a man, a woman, or a beast. If we agree with Cicero, and the faithful of every religious belief, that the soul persists after its "house" has been destroyed, we must conclude that the soul does not cease to exert, in death, an influence—for good or ill—on an animate body to which it is joined *by virtue of an extraordinary affinity.* This thesis, which, on face value, appears to be no more than the stuff of Gothic fiction, is, in actuality, an evolution of the idea of the *doppelgänger,* and neither more nor less strange than encountering one's double alive in the world.

And so it was that, in the year 18———, while on sabbatical in London, I fell under the evil persuasion of one William Boyle, lately of Crouch End, who, during the spring of that year, had murdered six young women living near the City of London. With nothing provable against their characters, they must be considered innocent victims of Boyle's hatred—of what, if anything, we can only surmise. The brass plaque affixed to the plinth on which his wax effigy stands—in the gruesome pose of a strangler—informs the visitor to Madame Tussaud's Chamber of Horrors, on the upper floor of Baker Street Bazaar, of the sensational, if brief, history of the figure's original:

WILLIAM BOYLE
BORN 1799
HANGED 1832
DID MURDER, IN COLD BLOOD,
SIX YOUNG WOMEN
IN THE PARISH OF HORNSEY

If ever a man or woman can be said to have fallen instantly in love or into a fit of madness, *I* fell under that dead man's malign influence. I did not, at first, realize the effect he, or his blasted soul, had on me. (It was very like love, strange to say, and also like madness.) I was not visited, all at once, with a compulsion to murder, in emulation of him. Rather, the hold he had on me—unbreakable like the adamantine chains of gravity—made itself felt, to begin with, in a curiosity impossible to resist. What was the nature of this curiosity? Boyle presented to the eye an utterly faithful *fac-simile* of myself, with the exception of a port-wine stain on his cheek, a stigma I had been spared by a more auspicious birth. I was not the only person to notice the uncanny like-ness between our two selves, apparent, notably, in the face of each. Indeed, I was not the first one to observe it.

I had been invited to Madame Tussaud's waxworks by a man with whom I had a slight acquaintance, owing to a mutual interest in the Neoplatonism of Augustine of Hippo. We had enjoyed a pleasant and instructive correspondence for several years prior to my trip to England. Indeed, it was Frederick Z——— who had made the arrangements for my first visit abroad. On an afternoon, conspicuous in my mem-ory for its rain and general dreariness, he offered to show me a few of the city's popular attractions and spectacles. (I confess to have been suffering, that day and the day before, from a surfeit of intellectual pleasure, amply provided by the library and the British Museum, and jumped eagerly at Frederick's suggestion as a means to allay my *ennui*.)

At quarter past two o'clock (after Welsh rarebit at the George and Vulture Inn, in St. Michael's Alley, Cornhill, a favorite of Mr. Pickwick's), I found myself viewing, with-out haste or method, minutely painted replicas of Voltaire,

Jean-Jacques Rousseau, and our own Benjamin Franklin, in addition to assorted royalty, cutthroats, and their victims, including those who had lost their heads to the guillotine. (Their death masks had served Marie Tussaud, the waxwork's artist and impresario, as models for the faces of her *macabre* figures.) I looked upon them with the interest a boy might take in a collection of butterflies: indifferent, or nearly so, to the colorful patterns on their wings but morbidly fascinated by the pin stuck through their abdomens. Still, I was glad to have escaped, for one afternoon, the library's fusty reading room and happy to have my mind lie idle and adrift. I had just come *vis-à-vis* with the notorious poisoner of Glatz, with the accordion name of Sophie Charlotte Elisabeth Ursinus, when Frederick called to me in no little excitement.

"Edward, come at once!"

Disconcerted to hear my name shouted among a crowd of persons, famous and infamous, in the grip of eternal inertia (eternal until the paraffin melts), I hurried to where my friend stood, mouth agape and finger pointing to the effigy of William Boyle, to whom the reader has already been introduced. A person of even meager sympathies will instantly apprehend the horror with which I beheld, in Boyle's face, the image of my own, except that his countenance was marred by a port-wine stain (as I have stated already in my deposition). The horror of that recognition was not absolute, however; there was an alloy of fascination, even *amour-propre*, in the gaze which I cast on that vicious and degenerate soul. (One sees, in the inadvertent application of the word "soul" to my dead and accursed double, how—even at our first meeting—I acknowledged, albeit unconsciously, the totemic power of his waxen effigy over my immortal portion.) Like the mysterious movement of the spirit through a living body or of a Mesmeric transmission through the ether, the connection between us was imperceptible. (A distant commotion of midges above a river may sometimes be neither seen nor heard by humankind; the hungry trout rises to them, nonetheless.) At that electric moment inside the Chamber of Horrors, Boyle and I were bound as surely as the Siamese twins Chang and Eng, which are among the medical anomalies to be found in Dr. Thomas Dent Mütter's collection, at Jefferson Medical College, in Philadelphia.

"It is utterly fantastic!" exclaimed Frederick, polishing the lens of his spectacles on his sleeve. "How can one explain so singular a phenomenon?"

I could not explain it, although I knew the concept of the *doppelgänger* from Shelley's *Prometheus Unbound* and Lord Byron's unfinished work, *The Deformed Transformed.* While in London, I re-read Mary Shelley's novel *Frankenstein; or, The Modern Prometheus* with especial dread, sensing in the doctor's relation to his misbegotten creature a similarity to that of Boyle's and my own. Until that instant, among the *bizarreries* of Madame Tussaud's, however, I had never encountered a *doppelgänger*, in flesh or wax, much less one who could—with good reason—claim me as its own! Had Boyle's painted likeness winked at me with a waxen lid, I could not have been more astonished!

"It *is* strange," I answered my friend with a deliberate, if unfelt, *sangfroid.*

In truth, to say that I was alarmed would be as wide the mark as to call a hawk a lark. I was terrified! Had a thunderbolt smote the ground nearby, I could not have been more shaken. I am not sure what compelled me to pretend otherwise to Frederick; I can only guess that I wished to keep my excitement a secret from him and any others who might discover my resemblance to a creature who was known, in North London, as the "Devil's Boil." There was about my terror, which was real, an equal element of *frisson*. I was like a boy who climbs to the top of an ancient oak tree and surveys the neighborhood in fear and wonder—*fear* of falling from so great a height and *wonder* at his daring. I sensed, in my *rencountre*, a perilous outcome. In the tensed muscles of my legs, I felt the urge to run from William Boyle, but was rooted to the spot. (I would speak of him thereafter as if he had not been hanged at Newgate, but stalked yet the lanes and alleys of Hornsey.) It might have been my own house, afire, with a wife and children inside, that I was viewing, with horror and an irresistible fascination, instead of the wax sculpture of a hateful dead man.

Frederick must have intuited something of the sort, because he laid a hand on my sleeve and—roughly, I thought—pulled me away from Boyle. He made an unconvincing show of amusement, and then he said, with an earnest fervor whose hidden import I could not mistake, "I've had enough of monsters! Let us visit the bears at Regent's Zoo. They ought to be more amusing than *these*." He waved his arm at what, in his mind, had assumed the status of an atrocity. "What do you say, Edward?"

"Yes, I am feeling much provoked by this chance encounter with myself."

Clasping my hand like someone wishing to confirm a palpable reality amid phantasms of delirium, Frederick expostulated, "You are a gentleman scholar from Philadelphia and not a murdering villain from Hornsey!"

We left Madame Tussaud's theatre of illusion and, for all my friend knew, I would spend the remainder of my stay in London in the reading room of the British Library. I am certain he would not have wished to know the truth: Each day I returned to the Chamber of Horrors and stood—enraptured and with an uneasy conscience—staring into the face of William Boyle, who, though he had not yet spoken to me, had ensnared me.

[There is, here, an interruption in the tale. The top third of the manuscript page has been ripped off, presumably by Poe himself, for what reason none will ever know, and the following clause struck out.]

... with the unerring instinct of a homing pigeon whose hollow bones contain an imponderable fluid responsive to magnetic north.

[The tale goes on from there.]

By my fourth visit to Madame Tussaud's, I had attracted the notice of a man dressed to impersonate Antoine Louis, inventor of the guillotine. (Although his name is eponymous with the instrument of execution favored by the French, it was M. Louis, and not Dr. Joseph-Ignace Guillotin, who conceived it.) The task of the impersonator, in powdered wig, cravat, and breeches, was to serve as the waxwork's *cicerone*, ushering visitors among the historical *fac-similes*, as if he himself had only recently been galvanized into life, in order to satisfy curiosity about their originals. His courtesy did not conceal his suspicion, which I could not fault, since my attention, during each of my later visits to the "chamber," had been paid exclusively to William Boyle. It was my habit to arrive, at about two o'clock in the afternoon, at his replica, given pride of place between two contemporaneous villains, both Bavarian: Andrew Bechel, fortune-teller and fetishist, and Anna Maria Zwanziger, who referred to arsenic poison as "her truest friend." Sitting on an ingenious contraption, combining a walking stick and a stool (known as "a museum chair"), I would give myself up to the contemplation of Boyle.

"Pardon me, sir," said "M. Louis," who had drawn up beside me and spoken before I had been made aware of him.

I looked at the man without comprehension, so enthralled was I to an alien power, one both secret and undeniable. "What is it?"

"I have seen you sitting here, by the hour, on four afternoons. . . ."

"Yes?" I asked irritably, wishing him gone about his business.

"I only meant to inquire whether or not you are in need of information," he said, giving me a sidelong glance.

"What kind of information?" I demanded.

He must have been inured to the vexation of visitors, for he continued affably. "I have made a study of William Boyle's crimes and will gladly tell you all I know of them."

I already knew a great deal about William Boyle. The reader will hardly credit me when I say that I had begun to receive, through the etheric currents that passed between my waxen double and myself, his thoughts and memories. (I say "waxen," but, in truth, it was Boyle, the man himself, who stood before me.)

The *cicerone* did not stir from my side. He grew restless. I knew then what he wished to ask me, but was too polite to say. I said it for him.

"No doubt, you have noticed the resemblance between us."

He took off his tri-cornered hat and mopped his brow, with a sudden nervousness that betrayed his ulterior purpose in having accosted me. "I have, sir."

"Strange, is it not?" I was enjoying his discomfiture.

"It is very strange," he agreed, stealing another look at me.

"It is this likeness which has brought me here these three afternoons since my first encounter with it. You can, perhaps, imagine my curiosity . . . my fascination."

He nodded in the affirmative, and I suddenly grasped an additional, more urgent, reason for my visits there: to purchase the plaster death mask from which Boyle's face had been cast in wax.*

[Poe inserted a second footnote here: "*Sub conservatione formæ specificæ salva anima.*" How is your Latin, Moran? If I remember mine, the epigram translates: "The soul is saved by the preservation of the specific form." To continue Poe's tale.]

"I should like to speak to Madame Tussaud," I said, drawing myself up to my full height, which, however, was not imposing. I attempted a supercilious manner and said again, "I should like to speak to her *now*."

Without another word, he escorted me to her *atelier*, knocked once upon the door, and went his own way, with what I imagined was a feeling of relief.

"Excuse me, Madame," I said, when she opened the door to me. "I wish a word with you."

"What is it you want?" she asked, after having resumed her place behind an armature, on which a lump of wax was waiting to be transformed into the head of a Roman emperor.

"I want to buy the death mask of William Boyle," I said, hoping my voice would not reveal emotions that were, at once, complex, poignant, and fearful. "I will pay anything within reason. I am not a wealthy man; I am only a scholar."

"The masks are not for sale!" she said sharply, but in a moment, she relented. "However, in your case, Mister——"

I gave her a false name.

"I will give you the mask."

"*Give it to me?*" This sudden turn of events had caused the wind to spill from my sail, so to speak, and I was, momentarily, becalmed. She knew, of course, why I wanted it. She was an artist and did not need to see Boyle and me standing side by side to realize that we were twins, in all but the stain on his cheek. She must have sensed, in my request, an urgency well beyond that of a mundane business proposition. "Why would you be kind—more than kind, munificent—to a stranger?"

"It pleases me."

And so, with my double's death mask inside my trunk, I sailed home to Philadelphia.

II

No sooner had I settled into my rooms on Ludlow Street than I went out-of-doors again, carrying the death mask inside a valise. I was acquainted with a man who worked in the county coroner's office, and I trusted that he would know someone with the requisite skills to produce a likeness of William Boyle's head in wax, clay, or plaster of Paris from his death mask. I was successful in securing the services of an expert, and, in two or three weeks' time, a *trompe l'oeil* re-creation of my double's head became the centerpiece of my dining-table, where I could study it to my heart's content. I did so with the avidity of an astronomer who has discovered a new planet.

I knew something of the sciences of phrenology and physiognomy, and, with my fingers, I would read his character, its aversions and propensities, until they became second nature to me. I would spend hours gazing at Boyle's countenance, which was as familiar as my own, my mind empty of all thoughts, save his. In time, I completed the mental transference that had begun at Madame Tussaud's. I now knew William Boyle as well as I knew my own self, because, in a very real sense, I was he and he was I. (Could "M. Louis" have whispered in my ear the history of William Boyle, while I was under the influence of his effigy? No—*I say no!* My knowledge of his perversities was too intimate and comprehensive.)

It was only then that I understood the reason for our having met, as if by chance, and the purpose—ordained by fiend or devil—of our affinity: I would continue Boyle's career, which had been curtailed by the hangman's noose. I would bring to Philadelphia the terror Boyle had let loose in London, wreaking havoc on the City of Brotherly Love. I would kill for motives he had yet to confide, if indeed he himself knew them. Whether my fate was to experience ecstasy or depravity, it didn't matter, so long as I followed Boyle's wishes.

And so, I, who had been a peaceable, even a meek man, sat at the dining-table, under the stern gaze of my master, preparing a list of victims, while the mantel clock ticked in the silence, like time's own great heart. The passing seconds fell all about me, a fine gray snow that was, in fact, only dust. As I wrote, I felt a sensation on the skin of my cheek, which, to the touch of my fingers, was hot. Having gone to the mirror, I saw that my face now bore the lurid disfigurement of a port-wine stain. I was not surprised to find it there. That night, when I lay abed waiting for Morpheus to descend, I pondered our fates—Boyle's and mine. If his blemish had been removed by the new surgery *before* he took to murdering, would his life—and mine—have been different? I had read an account in the *American Sentinel* of the repair of a hideous facial deformity, borne since birth by a young man named Nathaniel D———. Even now I could go to the surgeon, a Dr. Mütter, of my own city, and implore him to remove the stain from my cheek. But I did not want it gone!

[A clause follows—the beginning of a sentence which was to be the start of a paragraph, but Poe had not had an opportunity to continue before I made off with his manuscript. The tale ends here.]

No matter that he had left the manuscript unfinished, the story had shaken me. Pricked by nervous dread, I thought to throw it onto the fire as my mother wished and Savonarola, the fanatical priest, would have done had he been alive and his puritanical bonfires still raged. But they had been extinguished by tolerant men centuries ago, and I took my own dead fire as a sign that Poe's work ought not to be destroyed. Nevertheless, I would not give it back to him to finish. I felt a superstitious fear; completed, the tale might become a fatal lodestone, strengthening the magnetic affinity between my own murderous double and me. Already, I thought of him as a part of me, vile and unwelcome like a maggot in a piece of meat. I wanted to jump up and run to the hospital's incinerator and burn the tale together with gory bandages from the pit. But no, no, I mustn't!

I was on the horns of a dilemma, afraid to destroy Poe's story and just as afraid not to. The manuscript was a curse that might be visited on me if I burned it or if I did not. My mother may have been right in fearing that the smoke from the smoldering manuscript could cause the devil to appear, if not he, then a horde of glowering authors whose works had perished during the burning of the Alexandrian library. Like a voodoo curse, the manuscript might also overturn my reason unless I were to get rid of it. Either/or. The pit or the pendulum. In the end, I hid it underneath my bedroom's floorboards. I was sorry I'd taken the goddamn thing and wished I'd never met Edgar Allan Poe!

I passed the night in a hive of dreams. Next morning, I

retained mostly vague impressions from that troubled sleep. I recalled Ida as I had pictured her while I'd fumbled foolishly with the fat whore. I seemed to see Virginia Poe's sad porcelain face and remembered that I wanted very much to trace its lines and contours with my hands. I saw my mother on the stairs with a lighted candle in her mouth. In the most vivid of those jumbled scenes, I saw myself once again at the séance that Edgar and I had attended in January with Frances Osgood. We were holding one another's hands as we sat around the medium's table. I unclasped one of mine and laid it on Osgood's lap, and a bird, a pigeon, flew out from the collar of her dress. She swooned, and Edgar snickered. His mustache fell onto the table and wriggled there until Mütter impaled it with a specimen pin.

Poe's tale had put a torch to my imagination, turning its mazy, commonplace passages into Prince Prospero's lurid halls. I might have been stalked by the Red Death itself, so fine and inescapable was the net of Edgar's prose enchantment.

I knew the tale was dangerous, Moran, but I couldn't resist exhuming it from beneath the floorboards. I was drawn to it the way we are drawn to sin or to an evil that charms us. I would ponder Edgar's story, which was also mine, whenever I had an idle moment. Solitary during those weeks, I drank a good deal, as one does in hopes of forgetfulness. Sometimes the thought came into my head that I might be released from sin—strange words in this instance, but let them stand—if my house should burn down, through no fault of mine, but spontaneously, by a spark, say, jumping from Ben Franklin's machine—or from God's finger, the one that touched Adam and raised him from the mud. If only *He* would destroy Poe's infernal manuscript, I'd be saved! A lunatic's delusion.

TWO OR THREE DAYS AFTER I'D BURIED "The Port-Wine Stain" under the floorboards, Poe confronted me. *Confronted* is too strong a word for our encounter on the college roof. There was no evident hostility. He approached me—the better word—while I was feeding and watering the birds. I had been preoccupied by his unfinished tale and did not hear him enter the coop until his shoes crunched on the gritty floor. I turned in surprise and saw him standing in a shaft of weak March sunlight, alive with dust motes and down. By impulse, I picked up the manure shovel in case I should have to fend him off.

"Good morning, Edward," he said with disarming geniality.

I put the shovel down and faced him with more resolution than I'd previously been able to muster during our . . . trysts.

"Good morning, Edgar," I replied in kind.

"And how are your subjects—thriving, I hope?"

He picked a downy feather from the sleeve of his black coat.

"Tolerably well," I replied.

He kept his dark eyes fixed on mine; I held his gaze. He wiped the sole of his shoe—nervously, I thought—on the boot scraper. I took his nervousness as a triumph of my will. He must have realized his discomfiture, because he took a step toward me and frowned. He meant to appear menacing, but his mustache twitched comically as in my dream of Sarah Whitman's séance.

"Did you steal my manuscript?" he demanded.

If there'd been a clock inside the coop, its ticking would have echoed in the silence that followed his challenge. The time between one tick and the next would have seemed an age. In that silence and during that age, I'd have pondered my answer. Should I admit my robbery or pretend innocence? But no clock ticked; the moment was brief.

"I stole it!" I blustered.

My defiance seemed to stagger him. No doubt, he'd come prepared to hear an indignant or a frightened denial. I took a step toward him; he took one back.

"Why?" he asked without anger. I realized that I'd hurt his feelings—had wounded him—betrayed his idea of the friendship we two had shared—never mind the shocks he'd given me. "Why?" he asked again in perplexity.

"You had no right to use me as you did!" I stammered in a sudden gust of anger. "Again and again, you took advantage of me . . . used me—shamefully!" Anger had grown too hot for grammatical niceties. "Having me boxed up like a . . . sending me the skull . . . and now this *story*." I spat out the word like a rancid morsel.

"I dedicated it to you, Edward," he said, offended.

I laughed at the presumption. He believed that I'd be honored to have an Edgar Poe tale dedicated to me and that his offenses against me would be pardoned because of it! I turned my back. I heard the hesitation, the reluctance, that would have been visible in his stance had I been facing him. I kept my back turned toward him, and, in a moment, he left the coop.

I went downstairs to the exhibits room. I stood at the window and watched a teamster unload a heavy crate. I admired his strength and envied his ordinariness, although God knows what devils he might have had locked inside him. We are dirty windows, Moran; a little light passes through us—a candle's worth and no more. We are mostly blind to one another. All this time that I've been talking— what, I wonder, have you made of it and how much more remains that will be forever untold and unacknowledged?

Here, then, was the fatal crisis, Moran, when the fever rises but will not break. Here was anxiety raised beyond what can be endured. I wanted to be someone else but knew that it would make no difference if I were. We are beleaguered and estranged; we are, all of us, untouchables. I was a pallbearer for the funeral of all human feeling.

"Edward," said a voice.

I turned from the window but saw no one.

"Edgar? Holloway?" I called.

There was no one there.

On impulse, I fetched my doppelgänger's skull and sat with it at the table where I'd catalogued many another cranium that had belonged to a man or a woman once living and now dead, a being like myself who had raised a hand in greeting, in anger, or, perchance, in murder. This one, my evil twin's, had thought to kill or had been driven to it, only to have been killed in his turn. Like a good phrenologist, I felt the skull's irregularities: The prominence above the ear indicated anger. I played at physiognomy: The small chin told of a sensitive being whom the harshness of life might have overwhelmed and cankered. If I'd also had my double's hand, I'd have tried to read its naked palm; I'd have found, if only in my imagination, the line predicting a truncated life, a dangerous journey, a blasted heart. The nails would have been bitten in fear or envy or else broken by work or a life spent clawing out of some dung heap.

Under the influence of Poe's tale of the port-wine stain, I felt the flesh on my face tingle as it will when an eruption occurs—from a pore clogged by an ingrown whisker, for example. I went to the mirror above the sink and looked at my face. Moran, I swear to you, I saw a port-wine stain there! As yet, it was small, only the presage of what would come, in a short while, to cover my cheek—just as it had in Poe's execrable tale. I understood then that a consanguinity existed between the dead man, the murderer whose skull sat leering at me on the table, and myself. What he was, I must also be. What he did, I must, in my turn, do. You can't imagine with what horror I entertained the thought of my eventual overthrow. I returned to the table and took my twin's skull in my hands and gazed deeply into its eye sockets, where light was wont to arrive with pictures—pretty or not—like images carried on the beam of a magic lantern.

Where had they gone? Might they have wormed their way into me—into my brain with its furrows—eating, like worms inside the earth, into the sentient lump where my mind sits and broods? I strained to feel something not my own. I searched my memory for images, words, odors that had nothing to do with Edward Fenzil. In my vexed state of mind, I began to sense the pneuma of another being. Its *spiritus*. I'd been invaded by this other me, Moran. I was Lucien; he was Louis; we felt each other's pain. We were the Corsican brothers, jumped from the pages of Dumas père into Dr. Mütter's ossuary. Like them, we were joined—my criminal twin and I—by animal magnetism. My God, Moran, the thoughts that tumbled into my agitated brain that winter afternoon would have deranged the sanest man alive!

And then a mad conversation ensued—madder than the one I'd imagined among Mr. Bones, Tambo, and the Interlocutor—a catechism, an interrogation, between my self and my double's skull.

Did he have a name?

I've forgotten it. No, in truth, Moran, I refused to know it, like a woman who refuses to acknowledge a person in the street who has offended her. I did not want to know my other self's name! I feared that, by knowing it, I'd give my twin power over me that might—who knows?—have usurped me. *Me, me, me*—there is no way to tell my tale without seeming vain and self-absorbed. Forgive me, I never meant to go this far. I've admitted much I never said to Walt Whitman or Eakins or to anyone else until now. I must be in need of confession or a purge. A bloodletting, perhaps. The choleric humor must have swamped me in its rancor; must have pickled me, liver and lights. Unless Poe has settled his *spiritus* on me like an inheritance from where he lies moldering. After all this time, I thought I had escaped him.

To pick up the thread where I left off: I conversed with

the skull of my doppelgänger. *Conversed* is more apt for learned intercourse than a lunatic's debate.

> ME *(angry and fearful)*: What is it you
> want from me?
>
> SKULL: To size you up. *(Pause.)* To take
> your measure, then. By now, you real-
> ize the strength of the bond between
> us—the affinity, a word you seem to
> like. We have an ether in common.
> It's that which enables us to have this
> conversation.
>
> ME: I—
>
> SKULL: NOT I. *We.* And having said "we,"
> I might just as easily say "I," meaning
> me myself.
>
> ME: Who gave you the right to speak for
> me?
>
> SKULL *(amused)*: Who?
>
> ME: *What,* then.
>
> SKULL: You haven't a monopoly on our
> mutual identity. An identity until now
> apparently separate and equal. No,
> Edward, I can just as readily become
> you . . . drive you out . . . expel and
> destroy you.
>
> ME: I'll fight tooth and claw to be what I
> am.
>
> SKULL: What are you? You dust the doc-
> tor's shelves. You dispose of the bloody

messes he and the other gods make.
You yearn for a girl and fuck her fat
facsimile. You wander the streets,
confused and full of doubt. You drink
too much. You fall under the spell of a
madman. You let him use you for his
own purposes. You're a very flimsy idea
of a person, Edward. I, on the other
hand, know myself and my strength.
It would be nothing for me to take
your place. I would do it with no more
regret than having crushed a gnat
under my thumb. I could do it with the
same ease and untroubled conscience.

I was beginning to lose my mind. I might have already lost it. I felt the port-wine stain spreading across my cheek. Soon, I said to myself—while I still had a self to speak to—Soon you will be worse than a madman; you'll have become a character in a madman's fiction.

Don't misunderstand me, Moran: This that I'm telling you now isn't a fable of the old notion of the Bi-Part Soul, nor am I recounting the magnification to an unnatural degree of the empathic faculty or an inadvertent ventriloquism on my part. I hadn't thrown my voice into the skull; the skull had spoken to me—and for my ears alone—and I had spoken to it.

I had not seen Dr. Mütter enter the exhibits room, and I wouldn't have known he was standing behind me with a hand on my shoulder if he hadn't shaken me.

"For God's sake, Edward, what are you saying?" He looked at me as at a person in a fit. "What are you saying to that skull!" he cried.

Mütter hadn't seen a ghastly pantomime, but had overheard my part in a dialogue—his sense of hearing inadequate to the utterances of a talking skull.

I tore my hat and coat from the clothes tree violently enough to make it teeter. I ran up the stairs to the roof, intending to break the thread that tied me to a murderer's thoughts. I stood at the edge of the roof—it might just as well have been the summit of Mount Everest—and waited for the pendulum to decide my fate. I couldn't do it, Moran. For all my faint heart's bluster, I hadn't the courage to step out into the void.

Shamed by my cowardice, I went inside the coop and strode among the bickering birds, like Gulliver in Lilliput, and, with a fury I had not known before, I wrung their necks. A part of me was appalled; another part marveled at the sensation in my hands as, one by one, their gristly necks snapped and, with them, the thread—a slender one, no more substantial than a spider's—that had held them fast to the dirty floor and would have reeled them home in sunlight from the darkness of their wickerwork baskets. Did they feel what Holtz, or Heinz, had felt at the moment of surrendering his neck, for good and all, to a vengeful justice? It's a solemn thing to kill a bird, and I was sorry afterward.

Yes, yes, they were only birds. But it takes only a little more effort, a turn or two of the screw, to kill one of our own kind, Moran. Ordinarily, I'm as sensitive as an oyster, and my sympathies embrace even an injured bird. But that day, I could have out-Heroded Herod.

I was glad that Mütter hadn't followed me onto the roof. I might have thrown him from it. I could picture him falling in his purple velvet waistcoat with the gold filigreed buttons, the tails of a beautifully tailored cutaway flapping in his headlong rush to ground himself once more and forever to the earth.

I left the little scene of carnage—a miniature version of Ulysses' house in Ithaca after he'd slaughtered Penelope's suitors, or of Niobe's after the gods had expunged her seven sons and seven daughters for some Olympian slight. Classical metaphors, Moran, for our ignoble age. It was only then I noticed the satchel. Unaware, I'd carried it onto the roof and into the coop, set it down to strangle the birds, and picked it up again. I had not noticed the deadweight in my hand, possessed, as I was, by hopelessness and its underside, rage.

What was in the satchel?

Why, the skull, of course!

"You're not yourself, Edward," said my mother in that querulous tone of voice I hated. "You're distracted and snappish when you're not glowering at the fire or reading those infernal pages. That monster you call your friend has ruined your peace of mind and mine. I would forbid you to see him again, if I thought you'd listen."

If not myself, then who in the hell am I? I wondered.

"I won't see him anymore," I said with an involuntary shudder.

That shut her up, I can tell you! We were having dinner, boiled potatoes and some kind of stringy meat that appeared gray by the light of the oil lamps. It may have been gray, even in daylight. I beheld my plate with the disgust ordinarily reserved for the contents of a bedpan. I beheld my mother, with her sharp face, and my brother, with his jowly one, with a like distaste. Not that I didn't have affection for them.

Before my derangement, I'd have been happy to shovel the steaming food into my mouth and glad of their company after a day spent amid human wreckage brought by the tide of death into the college's exhibits room. But the memory of the pigeons—their little corpses on the floor, necks twisted evilly, tiny hearts stilled—made me despise Mother and Franklin both for the simple reason that at that moment in my history I despised myself. *That*, Moran, is the usual way of our species. Our brows are furrowed by doubt; our brains are furrowed by the struggle to think; our affections are a tangled skein impossible to unravel.

My mother lowered her fork, on which a piece of meat— once the exclusive property of a pig, a goat, or, who knows?, a dog; if dog, why not a rat?—was skewered. Do you know of a more revolting word than *meat*?

"I'm glad, Eddie. Will you go to church with me on Sunday?"

"My rehabilitation does not extend that far."

To my own ears, I sounded wonderfully arch. I might have been playing the villain in a melodrama.

"It will do you good," said my mother, whose ears were either deaf to irony, or plugged up with wax.

"I'm not interested in doing good, neither for my own sake nor anybody else's."

What a prig I was! What a smug little bastard!

"You ought to get out into the air more," she said, setting her horrible fork down on the plate so that it rang. "It's unhealthy, that job of yours, to be all day surrounded by monstrosities and deformities. They come of wickedness, Edward—wickedness and a sinful nature. You'll turn into a monster yourself if you're not careful."

If she'd been a Catholic, she would have crossed herself.

The skull of my doppelgänger sniggered from the leather satchel, where it was shut up in the dark. I looked at Mother and Franklin to see if they'd heard it. Franklin was noisily mashing a potato with a fork, while she fixed me with a stare whose censoriousness was undermined by myopia. I felt tempted to retrieve the skull from the front room and fling it apocalyptically onto the platter, whose leftover meat might have been mistaken for its brains.

"Franklin, why don't you take your brother with you tonight? He's out of sorts. He spends too much time with Mütter's horrors and with that horrible man Poe. It'll be good for him to get out among —"

The phrase "vulgar, coarse, and common men like you" hung unspoken in the air before us. She seemed embarrassed by it. My brother snorted.

Here was a twist, Moran! My mother had always tried to keep us apart, fearing my brother's low morals would corrupt me, the younger of her two sons. Franklin was twenty-four or twenty-five at the time and had had experiences consonant with his age, with his liking for gin and cards, and with the type of men with whom he rubbed shoulders on the docks.

"What do you say to that, little brother?"

"I'd be delighted!" I replied like a swank.

"Beer and a game of draughts won't harm you, Edward, so long as it's only small beer and you don't wager anything but matchsticks. Do they play draughts at Noonan's, Franklin?"

"Naturally," he said, with a wink for me, which she noticed.

"Be careful with your brother, Franklin," she said shrewdly. "He's not well."

"What do you have in the bag?" asked Franklin as we got into our coats.

"A severed head."

"It won't look out of place among the mugs who soak themselves at Noonan's trough."

We went to Noonan's taproom, on Catherine Street. I took the satchel with me. I felt my nerves unknit like an anchor cable as we sat at the bar, which was carved with the names of men who would make their marks in this way and no other, except for the lucky ones whose memorials would be chiseled on gravestones. Luckier still were those whose names and spans would be joined by the endearing, if not enduring, inscriptions BELOVED SON or BELOVED HUSBAND AND FATHER.

A dozen patrons, representing the stages of man's fall from grace, stood at the bar. They were hardworking men whom work had not ennobled. They wanted little enough. In this, they were like homing pigeons, which yearned for only a tiny corner of the world in which to roost. As I grew into a sublime state of intoxication, I saw my fellow drunkards through a lens that softened them and blurred their coarseness. I began to think them a fine and generous lot, the "camerados" Walt Whitman adored. Noonan croaked out a sentimental ballad. It was his saloon and his right, therefore, to make a fool of himself.

> All the dames of France are fond and free
> And Flemish lips are really willing
> Very soft the maids of Italy
> And Spanish eyes are so thrilling
>
> Still, although I bask beneath their smile,
> Their charms will fail to bind me
> And my heart falls back to Erin's isle
> To the girl I left behind me.

What happened after that was mostly hidden from me in alcoholic fumes and tobacco smoke, which fogged my brain as much as they did the dusky room. I recall staggering outside into an alley to piss, and when I'd found my way back to my empty glass, my brother was ogling the skull. No one else in the madly whirling room seemed to have noticed it, squat and stolid on the bar, but Franklin was entranced. I had few wits left, but enough to wonder if the skull might not have spoken to him.

"Franklin," I said, tugging at his sleeve. "Franklin!"

He looked at me and winced, as though my face were a

skull, too. He got to his feet unsteadily, shambled toward the door, and vomited in the vicinity of a cuspidor. What did not manage to fall onto the sawdust-strewn planks hit a Swede boatswain's shoes.

"Watch where you're spewing, you drunken lickfinger!"

He pushed my brother into a knot of mangy good-for-nothings, stewed road menders, by the look of their clothes, well on their way to blazes. Their golden voyage abruptly ended, they turned in indignation and stomped him with their dirty boots. To see poor Franklin lying on the floor like a dead halibut, I wept, believing he had passed beyond all mortal storms. He was, however, soused by gin, which had rendered him, if not immortal, at least unconscious.

We ought to drink a toast, Moran, to gin—the sovereign God-given general anesthetic!

I left my brother to the sawdust and his infamy. My skull and I—I saw no difference now between my own and one the dead man had carried on his shoulders—stepped out into the chill March night like Caesar on his way to subdue the Gauls or to the Senate to be slain by Brutus. I held tight to the satchel. In it was the incorporation of a universal fear that not even Jesus at Gethsemane could have denied. I carried the satchel like a bomb I might fling at—what? The massive lock on Eden's ancient rusted gate forever lost behind weeds and nettles? The impious Eschatologists numbing themselves with drink and ether against the coming on of night? Dr. Mütter's "Old Curiosity Shop," where a nature as malignant as the hunchback Daniel Quilp's has undone the wicked and the innocent alike? I swear, Moran, if I'd had a bomb big enough to destroy the world, that night

I'd have used it gladly. I was, you see, filled to overflowing with the most corrosive of solvents: hatred and self-pity.

There was a fine soft rain in the air that night. I watched the drops form and fall from my hat brim when I passed beneath the streetlights. After a while, which may have been long or short, I found myself outside the house where I had been betrayed by lust. "Found myself?" As if the invisible thread of a destructive desire or the desire for self-destruction had not reeled me in! I was just sober enough to mount the stairs of that sad house, but not enough to mount any of its sad women. I fell into a bed on the second floor. I dreamed of a table covered with a linen cloth, where raw meat erupted with maggots and gravy congealed into fat. Or maybe I dreamed it on some other night. Memory is notorious and tells its own tales. I heard a scream as I was dragged up from the fen of sleep by a large man whose breath smelled of onions.

"Get out," he said with menace. "If you can't leave by the stairs, you'll leave by the window!"

A woman, half-dressed and that half slatternly, had opened the satchel and screamed upon seeing my skull grinning up at her. It was her scream that had come to me in my sleep like the last cry of the damned. The man pulled me out of bed. I caught the briefest glimpse of my face in a mirror. The port-wine stain had spread during my night of abandon. The man rushed me down the narrow, creaking staircase and sent me flying into the street with a kick. The next moment, the second-story window was thrown open and first the satchel and then the skull were tossed out into the rain. Sitting on the ground with the skull balanced on my knees, I thought of Ida. No, there was nothing tragic in this farce; the night had been one long and humiliating pratfall. Unlike Will Shakespeare's "poor Richard," I did not "sit upon the ground/ And tell sad stories of the death of kings." I thought of Ida and shed maudlin tears for myself.

Why should love, of all emotions, be so difficult, Moran?

Did I ask my doppelgänger for his thoughts on the matter?

I may have, and the conversation might have been something like this. I might even have "blacked up" with wet mud daubed on my face to complete my mortification, for I had degraded myself as vilely as the notorious "Daddy" Rice on the minstrel stage.

> INTERLOCUTOR: Brother Bones.
>
> BONES: Yessuh, Mr. Interlocutor?
>
> INTERLOCUTOR: What do you know of love?
>
> BONES: What kind?
>
> INTERLOCUTOR: A man for a woman, and vice versa.
>
> BONES: Of all the varieties of love, tha's the one I know the least about.
>
> INTERLOCUTOR: Did you never love a woman, then?
>
> BONES: I misremember. Might have, once.
>
> INTERLOCUTOR: Why did you kill the shopkeeper? Was it hatred?
>
> BONES: "It is impossible to say how first the idea entered my brain; but once

conceived, it haunted me day and night. Object there was none. Passion there was none. I loved the old man." Tha's all I ever knowed of love as I understood the term (and Mr. Poe wrote of it in "The Tell-Tale Heart.") How's about you, Mr. Interlocutor?

INTERLOCUTOR: Ida . . .

BONES: You full up for her, suh?

INTERLOCUTOR: I was.

BONES: Full up wid love or wid hate?

INTERLOCUTOR: I can't seem to separate them anymore. You've poisoned me.

BONES: Has I?

INTERLOCUTOR: You put the idea of murdering into my head, and I can't shake it out again.

BONES: Murderin' who? Ida?

INTERLOCUTOR: Not Ida.

BONES: Dr. Mütter?

INTERLOCUTOR: Not him.

BONES: Holloway?

INTERLOCUTOR: No.

BONES: Edgar Allan?

INTERLOCUTOR: That's the one. *(Bones laughs.)* I never would've thought of it if I hadn't met you.

BONES: We was fated to meet. Our black hearts beat as one; our two brains have the mind of a hive. The thought of

murder was tinglin' in the nerves of my
hands when I strangled the old man,
and now it's in yours. We're like the
pride of Mütter's collection: the plaster
cast of Chang and Eng, Siamese twins,
who were born as such and died as
such. Only in between, they married
two sisters, so, presumably, they knew
somethin' we don't know about that
love you was askin' me about.

INTERLOCUTOR *(sadly)*: I'm to be a murderer, then?

BONES: That is your destiny, suh. I sees it
in your face.

INTERLOCUTOR: The port-wine stain, you
mean?

BONES *(shrugs)*: That and other things not
so easy to call by name. Cheer up,
suh. It could have been worse.

I didn't want that destiny, Moran. I knew it would be the
end of me as well as of my victim, Edgar Poe. To spill blood
or ink, it was all the same to him.

INTERLOCUTOR: Mr. Bones, what do you
know about death?

BONES: All there is.

INTERLOCUTOR: Which is?

BONES: Nothin'.

INTERLOCUTOR: Meaning what?

BONES: Nothin'.

INTERLOCUTOR: Nothing is nothing.

BONES *(laughs)*: Ain't that the truth!

INTERLOCUTOR: Have you had a glimpse of the life to come?

BONES *(uncomfortably)*: Might have . . .

INTERLOCUTOR: Any glory in it?

BONES: No, ain't much shine to it.

INTERLOCUTOR: Dark?

BONES *(shivers)*: Plenty dark. Dark as a grave.

INTERLOCUTOR: Any sign of a Savior thereabouts?

BONES *(laughs)*: Only the one on his door, sayin' GONE FISHIN'.

I found a piece of iron lying in the gray, withered grass and, with it, dug a hole—a grave—for the skull. It leered at me as I covered it over.

"Nevermore!" I shouted to it in my mind. I thought I heard the skull laugh from under the dirt, but maybe that was only in my mind, too.

The sky was beginning to lighten above the river; the drizzle had stopped. I threw the satchel into an ash pit and hurried toward Ida's rooming house while the skull sang a minstrel tune in the chill voice of Mr. Bones.

I won't be here long,
Oh, I won't be here long.
Oh, dark gonna catch me here,
Dark gonna catch me here.
Oh, I won't be here long.

Clothes dirty, hat gone, hair looking as though it had been threshed, I burst into the dining room, where Ida and the other boarders were eating their breakfast. I wore the ecstatic look peculiar to saints and lunatics. I'd seen something that needed saying but that couldn't be spoken—a thing neither uplifting nor glorious, but true notwithstanding. My wits deranged, I believed the ladies would put down their forks and spoons and hear me with the ears of people hungry for the truth. I'd glimpsed it in the dark while sitting on the ground, a japing skull in my hands. It had been only dimly seen—there'd been no shine to it, as Mr. Bones had said—but I'd clutched it eagerly because it had come, like a telegraph message, from the Other Side. For a moment, the scales had fallen from my eyes, and I could see the darkness plainly. I suppose it was this that had finally driven me insane, not that I knew I was. I would have needed to step outside myself to know it, and that is a thing neither the mad nor anyone else can do. We're all sentenced to the "Little Ease" between our ears, Moran. All of us are locked up for life in a prison of bone.

Ida gasped like a Christian lady whom a drunkard had mistaken for a woman of the streets, while her pious sorority let out various noises descriptive of an unpleasant astonishment. None laid down their forks and spoons, which they grasped as though their bodies had stiffened in a cataleptic trance. The utensils did not shine, either, being as plain as the Calvinists who supped with them. Ida found her voice and raised it in an unchristian and uncharitable howl thrown at me like a stone at the woman taken in adultery. I watched in fascination while her pretty face, made ugly by what could only be called hate, screwed itself into a hideous mask that might have graced the features of Kali, the Hindu goddess of death. The other ladies seated at the table appeared to have gone to sleep.

"What are you doing here, Edward? You're a disgrace to your mother and an offense in the sight of God! What've you been doing? You're covered in filth! You've dirtied the Turkey rug with your muddy shoes!"

She may have railed at me in those words or some others. My brain was soused and my wits were addled. I can't swear to memory's faithfulness. There may not have been a Turkish carpet on the floor; its heathen origin and bright pattern would likely have jarred the boarders' puritanical consciences. Whatever the truth of that night thirty-two years ago, Ida looked at me as if I were one of the Gadarene swine into which Jesus cast the demons that had deranged the wits of a madman. I was muddy enough to look as if I'd spent the night in a wallow. Perhaps the dirt on my face covered the port-wine stain, because Ida made no mention of it, although by its itch I knew it must be increasing, along with my ignominy.

I ate a piece of toast and swilled a cup of tea, which scalded my mouth and made me bellow. The ladies who'd fainted awoke and found a lunatic raging amid needle-worked mottoes enjoining piety and zeal hanging on the walls. Their teacups trembled.

A woman took up her spoon against me, flinging tea like holy water from an aspergillum. "Satan, begone!" she intoned.

"Satan, begone!" the others commanded in unison while,

from the parlor, came a thin-voiced harmonium played by either an unseen boarder or a ghostly accompanist. Each of the sisters piped the old hymn in a reedy voice set to a deranged metronome audible only to herself.

> Long my imprisoned spirit lay,
> Fast bound in sin and nature's night;
> Thine eye diffused a quickening ray—
> I woke, the dungeon flamed with light;
> My chains fell off, my heart was free,
> I rose, went forth, and followed Thee.

It was not their censure, but their caterwauling, that drove me from the house. Its shrill vibrations pursued me through the ether. I took refuge behind a brick wall not unlike one on the other side of the city, behind which the witless lived obedient to laws peculiar to themselves. Soon enough, I'd be joining them.

What should I do now? I asked myself, squatting like a wretched toad.

"Kill Edgar Poe," replied my skull from its tiny earthen catacomb with only the stone of itself to mark the place.

Idly, I wondered where the rest of me had gone and hoped the rats were not gnawing it—prayed that my remaining portion rested tranquilly in the early-morning light and would not be carried off piecemeal by the dogs. Would the tattooed rope encircling the name Edgar Poe be legible on my arm's yellowing parchment? I could only hope that my unstrung bones would somehow find their way into "Mütter's museum," there to gather dust for another boy to clean.

"Knock, knock," said the skull.

"Who's there?" I asked.

"Anna."

"Anna who?"

"Annihilation."

Yuk, yuk, yuk!

You look skeptical, Moran. My expulsion from the dining room might not have been so comical or Homeric as I've described it, but I do feel obligated to be entertaining, at least a little; I've not been particularly instructive. I'm telling a story, Moran, one of the uncounted omnibus of tales that compose the world. The poorest of them has the strength of an enchantment.

I hurried to Poe's house, armed with a knife from the boardinghouse table—the sharp one used to cut bread from the loaf. The good ladies of the house would have to use their claws.

I HAMMERED ON THE POES' front door like Alaric on the gates of Rome. Poe said that a gaudy figure of speech was a silk cravat around a dirty neck. He didn't say whether the truth lay in the plain thing or in its fancy. Mrs. Clemm opened the door as if I'd been a peddler of bits and bobs or evangelical tracts and not a wild man come to claim her nephew's life.

"Is anything the matter, Mr. Fenzil? You seem overwrought. Would you like some tea?"

I made no answer, but pushed past her into the front room. I confess I knocked the old woman down. Aghast, she shrieked, bringing the neighbors into the street.

"Where's Edgar?" I shouted.

"Not here," she said, settling her cap back on her head.

I ran upstairs and found Virginia rising from her bed in alarm. "Edward!" she gasped.

"Where is Edgar?"

In an ornate mirror hung above her dressing table, I saw the lurid face of a maniac. It was the face of my doppelgänger as I'd seen it in the morgue, only the port-wine stain was now twice the size of the dead man's.

"He's gone to Mr. Lowell's." She'd seized a hairbrush of ivory or bone from the bedside table. I suppose she thought to use it against me if I should lunge at her. Poor creature, her small hand trembled. "Edward, whatever's the matter?"

I turned and ran down the crooked stairs and out the door, leaving her to gape at the place where I had stood, a madman in the toils of his mania.

I arrived at the boardinghouse on the corner of Fourth and Arch, where the Lowells were staying. In my disordered mind, the transit from one place to the other seemed instantaneous. I might have been a speeding atom of electricity, for all I knew of the intervening streets. Rarely have I been so unaware of my surroundings—the space and time they occupy. I was that way during my first amputation and have been so during the "little death" that sometimes follows an excess of alcohol or ether. I'm not one of those who employ the term to describe the culmination of sexual congress. I stood in the street, beneath the reeling March sky, and felt an upheaval in my gut and brain.

Waiting for a streetcar, a man and a woman formed a tableau of ordinary life. I felt sorry for them, as one pities those who live in a lesser world of diminished intelligence and sensation. I had "lost my hold of the magnetic chain of humanity," to steal a line from Hawthorne. He, too, must have believed in Mesmer's theory, which spawned the metaphor. Figures of speech, like myths, outlive the science that precedes them.

You were in the war, Moran, and traveled through the West. You must have killed.

You have. I thought so. One can tell, you know; extremity of emotion confers its own red badge—let's say, a certain look. Your face has it, your missing eye aside. I don't need to be a physiognomist to know that you have taken a life.

Two lives? They've left their marks on you. Killing is a continental divide in a man's character: on one side, experience, which is just another word for guilt, on the other, innocence, which is guilt in abeyance.

No, no! But thought is prelude to the act, and it marked me, also, as you can plainly see. There was nothing to be seen on the faces of that young couple waiting for a car except stolidity. I mean to say that they looked perfectly ordinary. And what is the perfection of a commonplace existence but nothingness? And so I pitied them while I exulted in a heightened consciousness—the sensorium, if you know the word—that sharpened every perceiving organ and faculty. If I'd been on the college roof that day and the pigeons alive and gibbering, I could have understood their language, as we will when we reenter paradise, according to the mystic shoemaker Jacob Böhme.

There'd been a storm inside my head—that's a fair way of putting it—and it had blown itself out and, with it, the trash laid down by almost twenty years of ordinary life. I saw—no, I suffered lucidity. Yes—*suffered* it, Moran. I saw clearly what the man and woman stepping into the street-car did not, or Poe, either, for all his vaunted insight into the mind at its limits. My double would've understood me—perhaps he did understand, if the cable by which we were made fast, one to the other, still held in his under-ground hell or nothingness. I nearly called to the skull but forbore, having cunning enough not to betray my violent state of mind in the public street—as if it were not obvious from my demeanor and my tousled hair!

Finding the door to the Lowells' rooms unlocked, I entered without knocking and discovered James Rus-sell and Edgar at a large writing desk, each with a pencil poised above a manuscript. Lowell, who did not know me, uttered an involuntary cry.

"Who are you?" said Lowell, having recovered suffi-cient breath to sputter in astonishment.

"I know him," said Poe with more presence of mind than the poet and abolitionist had shown. "It's the young man I mentioned in relation to the case of the port-wine stain. What do you want with me, Edward?"

"To murder you," I said to great effect, I thought, while I brandished the sharp bread knife.

I thought Edgar showed remarkable restraint for the object of so dire a threat. Lowell had retreated across the room, where he cowered behind an armchair—a very comfortable-looking armchair made cheerful by a pattern of tea roses that, here and there, had been singed by fiery embers of tobacco. I told you I saw things with unusual clarity; you could say a preternatural one.

"Why do you want to murder me?" asked Poe in the most reasonable way in the world. "What have I done to deserve it?"

"You introduced me to my double."

"Yes, it is a dangerous thing to meet oneself in the person of someone else, especially when the other happens to be dead."

"He was a murderer!" I exclaimed. "He may be one still!"

Poe gave me an amused smile. His voice still calm, he said, "I'm afraid you've let your imagination run away with you."

Having grown weak in the knees, Lowell sat abruptly in the chair.

"Is it comfortable?" I asked perversely, but he gave no answer.

"Edward . . ." Poe was about to console me, or else make sport of me.

"You sent me his skull!" I shouted with a child's sudden peevishness.

"It was meant in jest, Edward. As a prank."

"I know its mind."

"Its mind?" My oracular tone must have confounded him.

"I think its thoughts, and it thinks mine. It has given

me the wish to murder. I've chosen you, Edgar. It's only right that I should have. Even after having met myself and spoken with my skull, I would still not have dreamed of killing if not for your story 'The Port-Wine Stain.'"

"You should not have taken my manuscript!" He was incensed by the theft of his writing more than by my threat on his life. You see how vain and self-absorbed a breed these artists are. "You had no right to it!"

"It was about *me*!" I shouted, loudly enough to rattle the windows in their sashes.

"'Seeking some unknown thing in pain,'" Lowell chimed, quoting one of his own lines.

"I took an incident and made it mine," Poe continued equably, but the strain of having to maintain his composure told on his face.

"He took you and made you his creature," whispered the buried skull.

"And try as I might, I cannot find the words to tell it again." Poe laid a hand on his heart and lamented, "My muse has deserted me."

What a miserable, conceited ass!

He implored in a woebegone voice, "Please be so good as to return my story."

"I burned it," I said, gloating.

"Then it's lost forever."

"Evermore," I intoned. "It left me this to remember it by."

"What?"

"The stain on my cheek!"

"There's nothing there, Edward. You're imagining it. I fear you've lost your mind."

I lunged at him. The knife was large, and I'd have run him through if not for the timely intervention of a policeman called to the scene by a woman in the rooms opposite. He knocked me senseless with his truncheon.

Philadelphia, March–September 1844

I awoke in what was called, at that time, the Asylum for the Relief of Persons Deprived of the Use of Their Reason, maintained by the Society of Friends, in Frankford, northeast of the old city. How I'd arrived, by what conveyance I'd been whisked there, I could not have said. The chamber where I lay was narrow and chill; the windows were barred, the walls whitewashed and equipped with manacles for the better management of the guest. Thankfully, my brainstorm had subsided, making them unnecessary. I would not have worn them with any grace. After what may have been an hour or only minutes, an attendant appeared before me with a bowl of gruel. I wondered if I had not somehow fallen from Poe's tale into one by Dickens. But the attendant, whose name was Bruno, was kind, and during the six months and a little more that I was at the asylum, I was never abused.

We, the inmates, were treated according to the enlightened practices of our modern age, not as if we'd been possessed by devils, were being chastised for iniquity, or had had our wits turned by a cerebral inflammation or a lesion on the brain—the latter maladies once believed to be the universal causes of madness. Our reason had been overwhelmed by a perversion of the sensorial functions through which the mind expresses itself. The brain acts wrongly, and the result is a deranged intellect or feeling. The cause of mental alienation none can tell, because no one understands yet how the brain acts as the instrument of the mind. The great principle in the management of insanity, where there is no physical cause, is to direct the mind toward normal trains of thought and states of feeling, by which healthful actions can be excited and reinstated in the brain.

To this end, we were permitted to walk unhindered within the asylum walls, to breathe freely out-of-doors, to enjoy and cultivate the gardens, aesthetic interests, and the manual arts. We were not ourselves free, of course; the walls, bars, restraints, and the segregation of the two sexes were constant reminders of our confinement. But we learned to regulate our thoughts and emotions, so that, for all but the incurable among us, reason was eventually restored and we were allowed to go home. I didn't object to being there. I was a model inmate—tractable and affable—and never acknowledged, by word or gesture, that I bore the port-wine stain on my cheek.

Edgar visited me once. He forgave me, he said, for having destroyed his manuscript, and he presented me with an autographed copy of his newest published work, *The Prose Romances of Edgar A. Poe.* James Lowell visited me shortly afterward and gave me a copy of his new book, *Miscellaneous Poems,* also signed. The conceit of some writers who think their books sufficient to cure the woes of the world and the wretched people in it! Ida also visited me, once, making me a gift of *Institutes of the Christian Religion*, written by John Calvin in 1536—not signed. I was sick of books, stories, and of all who feel obliged to inflict them on the world. I consigned them to the netherworld beneath my cot, next to the bedpan.

At least once each week, Dr. Mütter visited the asylum. I called it the "seminary" because dark minds were remade there. He brought me tobacco for my pipe and would always offer me a drink of brandy from his flask. For these useful gifts, I was grateful, and grateful still more for his goodwill. It was by virtue of his generosity that I was a patient of the Asylum for the Relief of Persons Deprived of the Use of Their Reason instead of locked up in the charity hospital for the insane poor. The asylum was a private institution. Dr. Mütter was one of its patrons and paid the cost of my maintenance and cure from out of his own pocket. When I had recovered my wits and was restored to life as it is generally lived, he gave me back my old job as his assistant, and, as I've said, in years to come he would see me enrolled in and graduated from the medical college. Dr. Mütter was my great benefactor, and I was sorry for the unkind thoughts I'd had of him. I mourned him when he died in '59 of the gout. His remains did not end up in jars or under glass for boys to dust, but are entombed in the family vault in Charleston.

I remember one conversation we had in the azalea garden just inside the asylum's main gate. It was early May. The bushes were scarlet. The new grass underneath the dogwood trees was white with blossoms brought down by recent rain. We sat side by side on an ornamental iron bench and watched the robins tug up worms from the sodden earth.

"The mind gives up its secrets as reluctantly as the ground does those worms," he said in the gnomic manner that I very much used to resent. It pleased me now, however, to hear him take the roundabout. I waited for him to come to his point; I knew he had one. Dr. Mütter was never anything less than serious where the body or the mind was concerned. He was an eminent doctor, surgeon, teacher of medicine, and connoisseur of its oddities. "Your mind has suffered, Edward, and I feel partly to blame."

His contrition surprised me, Moran!

"I should not have thrown you and Poe together as I did. I should've known better than to encourage a friendship with a man whose own sanity was balanced on the edge of a knife. It was partly for your own good, but mostly for mine: I was curious to see the effect he'd have on you. I introduced you to an unstable element, and this is the result of my recklessness."

His roving eye took in the asylum and, here and there on the grass, persons ensnared in the various phases of lunacy. It was easy to imagine them as little boats set rocking by the sea's local disturbances—the sea's entirety drawn by the moon's own animal magnetism, causing the "moon sickness," which had brought us there. None of these airy thoughts occurred to me then; my mind, even before it had become obscured, was largely unformed and unused to speculation. It lacked . . . subtlety, the devil's gift to man, as wonderful and damnable as fire.

"His story was stronger than yours, Edward," said Mütter in conclusion.

Look out the window, Moran, at the people in the street. Smiling or frowning at one another or, more likely, buried in a private dream—a dishonorable fantasy, perhaps—rarely do they ever sense the spirit that moves them this way or that. And if they do sometimes sense it, they delude themselves into believing that it is their own that moves them. We tell ourselves a story we call our life.

I've come to believe that the world is papered over with stories. The most convincing of them become, for each one of us, reality. I knew a man in the asylum who believed he was an adjutant on Winfield Scott's staff during the War of 1812. He would be executed by the British, he told me, at the Battle of Lundy's Lane, on July 25, 1814. On that day in July—in *1844*—he hanged himself. He died believing he was in another man's story. His mind was deranged, the story untrue for him, but the rope was real enough to make it true. My double's story very nearly did me in. But I got the better of him, and, lately, I've been able to make him do my bidding.

See what I have here, Moran, in this silk pillowslip. He likes the feel of silk, you know, and I see no reason not to make him comfortable.

Yes, it's my old skull, the one I buried years ago. Recently, I dug it up. It was dirty, like an unearthed potato, and I had to scrub it clean. There was something green sprouting from the socket. I'd like to dig up Edgar Poe and talk to him. When he was alive, I didn't appreciate his gifts. He was the object of my first powerful attraction and the author of a second, greater one. I've been fortunate in my life to have known two men endowed with superior minds: Edgar Poe and Thomas Dent Mütter—both deceased.

Yes, yes, Moran! I speak to the skull, and it speaks to me. Handsome, don't you think? You can almost see it smile. It lacks only a layer of skin over the bone to prove its resemblance to me. More than an uncanny likeness, it would be a faithful copy. You'd see a port-wine stain exactly like my own. Eakins was kind not only to make me appear younger in his painting but to omit my disfigurement. Everyone pretends there's nothing there. I would not have believed people could be so sympathetic.

Not that I mind the mark anymore. I've lived with it for such a long time. The stain has become part of me; you could no more separate it from me than you could a bruise from the skin of a pear. Dr. Mütter tried—that is, he pretended to. He thought that a pretense of the restorative surgery in which he excelled would remove the monomania from my mind. I went along with his fraud for my future's sake, and when I awoke from the oblivion of an ether sleep and beheld my face in the mirror, I cried in my happiness. The tears were crocodile, and the port-wine stain had been as vividly present in the mirror as before. No surgeon's knife or mesmerist's power of suggestion can remove it. A counterstory might, but who is there to write one? I had no wish to return to the asylum, and I understood that normality dazzles those who are afraid to appear different from their neighbors. And so it has been. I've kept the secret locked up—here—inside my brain and inside this skull, whose gaze I still find riveting. No one has ever heard a complete account of my strange and eventful history until now.

What do you think, Moran? Have I told it well? Are you convinced of its truthfulness?

I might write it up as a reminiscence. I've written some factual accounts of the war. My book *A Field Surgeon's Notes* is in the Jefferson Medical College library. I wonder what Dr. Mütter would have said to that. I dedicated it to Walt Whitman so that he'd be sure to read it. He praised its poetical style. Yes, I really ought to pen an account of our meeting. Maybe I'll include "The Port-Wine Stain" as an apology to Edgar for having robbed him of his manuscript. His story would help mine to be published—don't you think?

You're leaving, Moran?

By all means, you don't want to miss the exposition. Be sure to visit the Army Post Hospital and see Eakins's great picture of Dr. Gross's clinic. When you stand in front of it, look for me among the young men sitting bemused in the painted darkness. But hold fast to your own story, Moran, because it's all too easy to become lost in someone else's.

There are certain themes of which the interest is all-absorbing, but which are too entirely horrible for the purposes of legitimate fiction.

—"The Premature Burial," E. A. Poe

Acknowledgments

My gratitude remains constant for those who have been steadfast in their devotion to me or to my work (they are, to my mind, indivisible): my wife, Helen; my children, Meredith and Nicholas; their spouses, Andy and Alexis; my mother, and (felt even now) my late father; as well as my publisher (and friend), Erika Goldman, and extended family at Bellevue Literary Press—Jerome Lowenstein, M.D., Leslie Hodgkins, Crystal Sikma, Molly Mikolowski, Joe Gannon, and Carol Edwards.

I ought not to forget to acknowledge the past American literature that, in recent years, has nourished me and my own attempts at contributing to it. It bears discovering or, as in my own case, rediscovering, if not for its relevance, which readers of my own time may dispute, then for its expression of the mind of its age, whose thoughts have gone toward the making of our own. I would not wish to be a literary conservationist, nor would I be a satirist. I would hope to be a twenty-first-century writer of American novels that speak to my own time through the literature that preceded them and, inevitably, give them shape and substance.

I acknowledge a debt to the historical record and ask forgiveness of those who will see in this novel certain liberties taken with it. Most flagrant of these instances may be my having brought forward, in time, the year of Poe's first meeting with Sarah Whitman (from 1848 to 1844). Dickey's suicide is another case of license taken. While I have been mostly careful of fact, I have written a fiction clad in history for the sake of verisimilitude. Mr. Poe, I beg your pardon for this concession to storytelling and also for my having borrowed some of your words and for having given you and Dr. Mütter mine to mouth.

Much of the text for the paragraph concerning the cause and treatment of insanity was taken verbatim from *Proceedings on the Occasion of Laying the Corner Stone of the New Pennsylvania Hospital for the Insane, at Philadelphia, Including the Address by George B. Wood, M. D., Senior Member of the Medical Staff of the Pennsylvania Hospital, etc. etc.,* published in Philadelphia by T. K. and P. G. Collins, Printers, 1856. I found this informative pamphlet in the digital collection of the US National Library of Medicine.

Regarding form and influence, my use of an Interlocutor and end men has more to do with John Berryman's *Dream Songs* than to a discredited minstrelsy. I ask my contemporaries to pardon it and also my use of certain nouns and pronouns that are unacceptable in our own era but were common usage during the years when my narrator was flesh and a living voice. I can only wish that the vices of the past had not survived into the present, which seems—in Berryman's words—a "funeral of tenderness." I can only hope (forlornly) that virtue—a word so old-fashioned as to sound ridiculous to our ears—will shed a benign influence over us through the "imponderable fluid that is everywhere present in the universe."

ABOUT THE AUTHOR

Norman Lock is the award-winning author of novels, short fiction, and poetry, as well as stage, radio, and screenplays. His most recent books are the short story collection *Love Among the Particles*, a *Shelf Awareness* Best Book of the Year, and two previous books in The American Novels series: *The Boy in His Winter*, a re-envisioning of Mark Twain's classic *The Adventures of Huckleberry Finn*, which Scott Simon of NPR *Weekend Edition* said, "make[s] Huck and Jim so real you expect to get messages from them on your iPhone," and *American Meteor*, an homage to Walt Whitman and William Henry Jackson named a *Publishers Weekly* Best Book of the Year.

Lock has won The Dactyl Foundation Literary Fiction Award, *The Paris Review* Aga Khan Prize for Fiction, and writing fellowships from the New Jersey State Council on the Arts, the Pennsylvania Council on the Arts, and the National Endowment for the Arts. He lives in Aberdeen, New Jersey, where he is at work on the next books of The American Novels series.

BELLEVUE LITERARY PRESS is devoted to publishing
literary fiction and nonfiction at the intersection of
the arts and sciences because we believe that science and the
humanities are natural companions for understanding the
human experience. With each book we publish, our goal is to
foster a rich, interdisciplinary dialogue that will forge new tools
for thinking and engaging with the world.

To support our press and its mission, and for our full catalogue
of published titles, please visit us at blpress.org.

BELLEVUE LITERARY PRESS

New York